A GATHERING OF EVIL

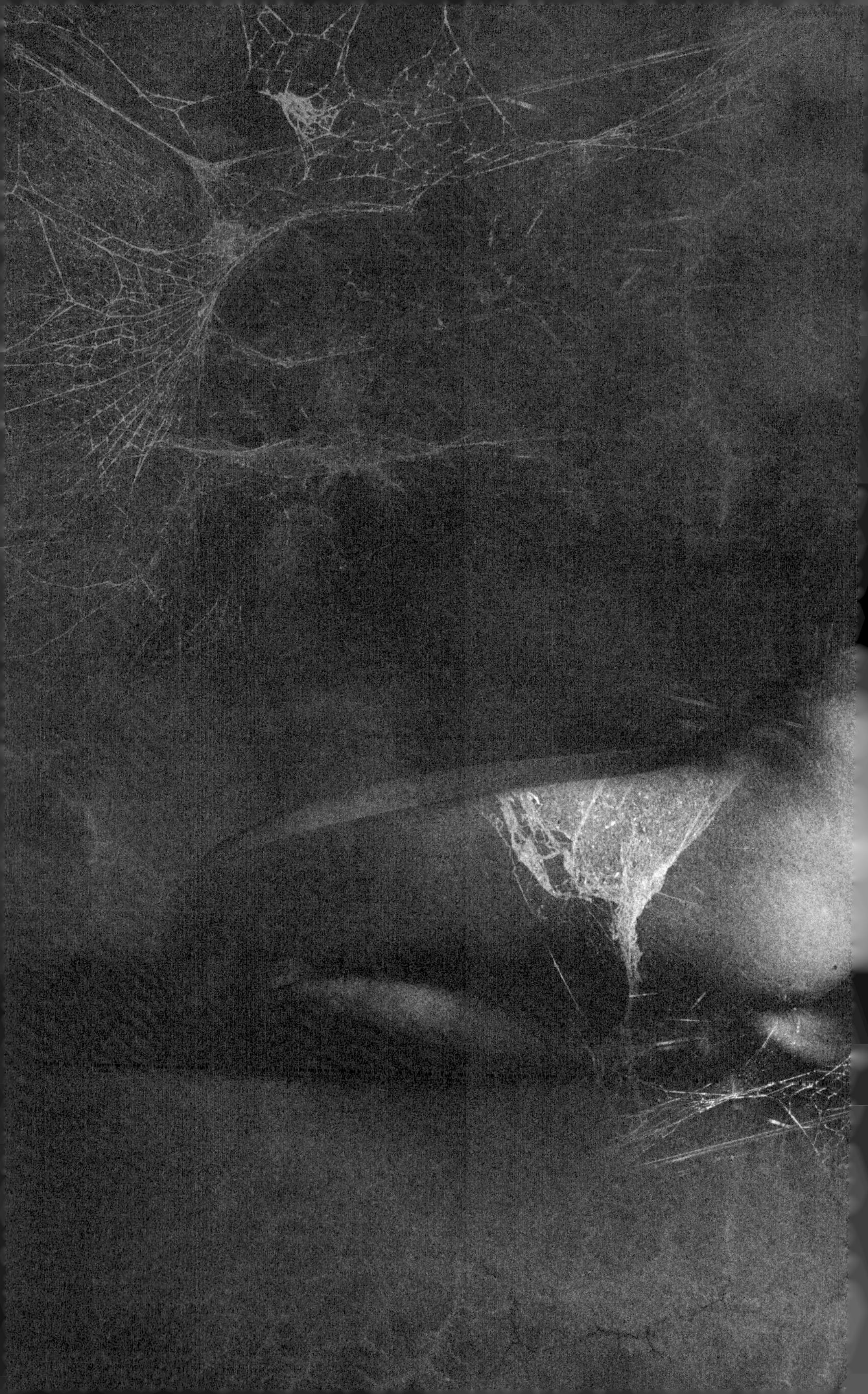

A GATHERING OF EVIL

GIL VALLE

First Red Room Press Trade Paperback Edition January 2018

Edited by Brian Whitney

Cover model photography by Marcus Ranum
Design by Sig Evensen, inkubusdesign.com

ISBN 13: 978-1936964055

Visit Red Room Press on the web at:
redroompress.com
facebook.com/redroompress
twitter.com/redroombooks

RED ROOM PRESS

WWW.REDROOMPRESS.COM

ALSO BY GIL VALLE

The Social Catalogue of #Prey (Red Room Press)

Raw Deal: The Untold Story Of NYPD's "Cannibal Cop"

PROLOGUE

MONDAY JUNE 12, 2017

Howard Helton nodded to the doorman as he left his apartment building. Lately he hadn't felt like talking to people much. The late Spring morning warmth refreshed him as he made his way to the Starbucks a couple of blocks away from his building on the Upper West Side of Manhattan.

"Tall Pike?" the cute young blonde asked him with her sweet, mellifluous voice at the cash register.

"You got it Brittany. Thanks," Howard replied.

He pulled out a five-dollar bill and watched her get his order. She always seemed so happy, clearly loving life and everything that it had to offer. She came back with his coffee and a beaming smile.

"Keep it," he said as he handed her the money.

"Thanks so much. Have a great day!" Brittany responded.

God damn, she would be perfect, he thought to himself. He thought that about a lot of attractive, young women.

Howard walked past his apartment building and into Riverside Park, which, for the most part, was all he ever did anymore. He was three years retired from a long career on Wall Street as a risk officer. He had a lot of money saved, but no one to share his life with. Sometimes he was overcome with depression when he saw happy families while on his strolls. He felt so empty when he saw husbands with their wives and children. He'd always been so career-driven that he'd never realized how fast life would pass him by. Now suddenly here he was at seventy years old, and he was never going to have that life. He was alone and would stay that way.

As usual, he sat on one of the benches that flanked a long walkway along the Hudson River and sipped his coffee, watching a host of people go by. Some were walking dogs, a few people his age out for a breath of fresh air, and a lot of beautiful women jogging. He liked watching them the most.

There really are so many fucking beautiful women out here. How are they going to choose?

He'd wondered that countless times over the last year and a half, but *today* as he thought about it, he felt his phone buzz in his pocket. When he read the short, direct message, time seemed to stop. He read it six times. Even then he still couldn't believe it.

He calmed himself as much as he could, then got up and scuttled back toward his apartment building. He dumped what was left of his coffee in a garbage bin and zeroed in on the front door. He was almost hit by a car as he hotfooted across the street. After all of this time waiting, ending up in the hospital now would have been terribly anticlimactic and disappointing, to say the least.

He was more careful now. His heart was pounding. He entered the building, ignored the doorman and headed straight to the elevator bank. He pressed the "Up" button repeatedly and noticed that he had an erection. When he got into the elevator and pressed the button for the seventeenth floor, he read the short message again.

It's really happening. Holy shit. It's really *happening.*

He had his apartment key in his hand as the elevator door opened on the seventeenth floor. His exhilaration caused him to struggle a bit with the lock, but he finally got inside and locked the door. He went to his computer and logged into the secret, secure website that only a small number of people on the planet knew about. He was so excited that he had to unbutton his pants. He clicked on the newest topic from the administrators.

The content of the newest message provided the details for the event. He had done what was required to get on the list—it was quite simple but understandably necessary—and now he was formally invited.

At his age it was the only thing he had left to live for. The event was tentatively scheduled for Monday, July seventeenth, about two and a half hours northwest of New York City.

Tentative for obvious reasons.

He skimmed through the rest of the message. He would read it more carefully later, but he took note of the due date for the bids to the administrators. The highest bidders would be allowed entry into the event. He wasn't worried about that. He would bid more than enough. What he was really interested in, what he longed for, was in the two attachments with the message.

The first attachment was titled "Target #1." It contained pictures of a woman who clearly was unaware that she was being photographed. There were thirty photos of her taken on different days and in different settings, and quite a bit of personal information to supplement the pictures. He liked that. He wanted to know a little bit about who she is in life. Hardly aware of what he was doing, his hand moved to his crotch and he slowly jerked off while reviewing the photos. She was white, with black wavy hair and appeared to be in her late twenties or early thirties. She looked fairly tall and healthy, maybe just a few pounds overweight. She wouldn't win a beauty pageant, but she was attractive enough for what was planned. Howard had to concede that she was perfect.

Mmm. She is a great *selection.*

He opened the second attachment. "Target #2" was prettier than the first girl and appeared to be tall and in her mid-twenties. She was also white with shoulder-length light brown hair, and apparently in great physical shape. "Target #2" was obviously someone in the corporate world. Most of the pictures were taken in what was clearly Manhattan, and in many of the photos she was wearing business attire. There were also photos of her jogging in another area of the city. It was evident that she was healthy and took great care of herself.

They have *to get her. They have to get them both.*

He continued masturbating while looking through both sets of photos, imagining the upcoming events of July seventeenth, when these two women would be incorporated into his own lifelong sadistic sexual fantasies. He closed his eyes and imagined how each one would look naked. He imagined how each one would sound screaming. He imagined the sensation of sharp metal on a woman's flesh.

He was old and alone, but had his life turned out differently, he might never have found the administrators of this website, and for him that was a damn good consolation prize. On July seventheenth, if everything unfolded as planned, he thought that he could eventually die a happy man.

The same could not be said for those two women.

CHAPTER 1

MONDAY OCTOBER 17, 2016

"Okay, Doctor McConnell. Doctor Kramer is ready for you."

"Thank you."

Sarah McConnell exhaled slowly as she walked with the receptionist down the hall towards Dr. Kevin Kramer's office. Her heels clanked with each step. She was dressed in full business attire, which always made her feel uncomfortable and ridiculous. She hadn't thought she would be so nervous for the job interview, but knew it was because she really wanted this to work.

At twenty-nine years old, she was ready to settle down, and hoped this opportunity could turn into a long-term career. She was a lifetime New Yorker, born and raised on Long Island, and had graduated from Columbia University with a degree in animal science and a 4.0 grade point average. Her passion for animals had been formed at an early age, when her parents—both doctors—bought her a kitten when she was a little girl. From that moment on, she knew that she wanted to work with animals when she grew up. It wasn't until veterinary school at Cornell University that she zeroed in on what exactly she wanted to do.

After her second year at Cornell, she took a class trip to a national conference in Missouri for top graduate students in the field of animal science. There, she had an opportunity to network and gain valuable hands-on experience at the Kansas City Zoo. She had once considered a profession as a zoologist working with zoo animals, but after the trip to Missouri decided that a career in veterinary medicine caring for domestic house pets would be better suited for her.

She graduated Cornell near the top of her class, earning her Doctorate in veterinary medicine. Through it all, Sarah was extremely extroverted and always made time for fun. She worked hard at school but never took anything too seriously. She loved living up to the Irish stereotype by hitting the bars at least once a week. She never had problems making new friends, and she still kept in touch with her best friends from elementary school. She was the kind of person everyone wanted in their lives. She was happy-go-lucky and sincerely believed in the goodness of humanity.

As graduation presents, her parents bought her a car and a small house not too far away from them on Long Island. She was hired right away as a veterinary assistant at a nearby small animal clinic. It was pretty slow work and the pay was decent for someone just starting out, but she knew she could do better.

She stuck around for the experience for three years, until she came across a job opening at a fairly new animal hospital on the Upper East Side of Manhattan. They were looking to expand their hours to midnight to accommodate the working residents in the area, and they needed a veterinarian to run the later shift. The hours weren't going to be ideal, but Sarah sent her resume in and she was called right away for an interview.

"Doctor McConnell, come on in. Thank you so much for coming."

Dr. Kevin Kramer welcomed Sarah in with a handshake and invited her to sit with him at a small round table in one corner of his office. She had looked him up on the Internet before coming just to get a feel for what to expect. He was very well accomplished. His graying hair was combed over to the side, and Sarah thought that he looked good for a man in his fifties.

"Thank you for the opportunity! It's so nice to meet you," Sarah replied as they sat.

"I hate talking to people from across that big desk. I hope you don't mind. This feels a little more intimate and relaxed for me. I hope you're not nervous, by the way."

Sarah nervously laughed as she fished for a hard copy of her resume from her bag and handed it to him. "No, not at all. And I agree. I very much prefer the smaller table."

"Wonderful," Dr. Kramer said as he put his glasses on and reviewed her resume. "This is all very impressive stuff. May I call you Sarah?"

"Yes of course."

"Good, and you can call me Kevin. Now, you are obviously very qualified, as shown by your educational background and you seem to have had opportunities to sort of bring people together. You know that I'm looking for someone who would be in charge of a staff here, so could you expand a bit on your experiences where you've had any kind of leadership position?"

Sarah began by talking about her position as a resident assistant at Columbia, rattled off peer groups she had organized both at Columbia and Cornell, and finished up by mentioning her experience volunteering at Habitat For Humanity. That technically wasn't a leadership gig, but she figured that prospective employers liked to hear about volunteer work. She knew that Kevin was impressed, and she felt more relaxed now. He nodded in approval, and they went back and forth with a few more rote questions. Kevin asked her about her experience with handling the owners of sick animals on the brink of death. Sarah was prepared for that question, undoubtedly the most heartbreaking part of her job.

"For most of us, that is clearly the most difficult part of being a veterinarian. I also understand that for them, the owners, it's one of the hardest decisions they have to make. I always try to tell them that it is okay to cry, and I tell them it's okay to hurt, but then I try to get them in a place where they might be able to focus on and remember the positive moments, and that their pets undoubtedly lived good and happy lives. And that's all you can do as a pet owner. I just try to make that heartbreaking moment as peaceful as I can."

She knew she'd aced the question, and she felt like she was in.

"Now, the hours obviously aren't ideal. As you know, Monday through Friday from four to midnight. This is a very affluent area and a lot of people work, so I anticipate that most of our clients would be coming in during those hours. Can you make that work for you?"

"Definitely. I mean, I prefer it busy anyway. I am passionate about this career because I love animals but I also want to help people. I'm a hard worker, I'll treat the staff here fairly and with respect, and the hours are not going to be an issue for me."

"Great, Sarah. How about the commute? You okay there?"

Sarah laughed and said, "I have a car but I would never drive in the city. The Long Island Rail Road isn't far from me, and with these hours it would never really be crowded. When I'm going into the city for work, people will be leaving the city. So that's totally fine."

"Okay then. Let's talk salary, and then I hope you'll accept my offer to join the team. I think you'll bring so much to our office, Sarah."

* * *

When Sarah left the building she felt like she was walking on air, instead of the crowded New York City block. She pulled her phone out, opened the Facebook app and posted a new message to her timeline:

"Just got hired at a dream job! I start next Monday! So excited :)"

She took a longer route to the Subway station so that she could call her parents and tell them the good news. She started with her father.

"Hey, sweetheart. How did it go?"

"I got the job! I start next Monday!"

"Alright! Way to go honey. I knew you would. They have to be very smart people there, and the only smart thing to do was to hire you."

"Aw, thanks Daddy. Yeah, they were really nice. I'm so excited. And the salary? More than double what I'm making now."

"Really? How much?"

"One-hundred and forty fucking thousand!"

"Wow, sweetheart! That's incredible. Well, you deserve it. More than anyone, honey. Let's celebrate soon."

"Yeah, definitely. Let me just see what else is going on with Allison and the gang. They'll want to do something nice too."

"Right, well let me get off the phone then. I'll call Mom and tell her, don't worry about that. Congrats again honey."

"Thanks! I'll see you and Mom later."

After Sarah hung up, she saw that she already had fifteen notifications on Facebook; a combination of "likes" and congratulatory comments. For the first time, she felt that all the Ivy League school work was worth it. She smiled again when she thought about her salary, then she snapped back to attention when she got a text message from Allison, her best friend since the third grade.

"Congrats on the job! When u wanna go drinking bitch?"

Sarah laughed and replied, and the two women chatted for a few minutes and made plans to meet up that night at their favorite dive bar in Brooklyn near Allison's apartment. Allison would tell some of the other girls to come out too.

Sarah descended the steps into the Subway station to begin the journey back to Long Island. She would deal with her current employer and the process of resigning tomorrow. She wasn't looking forward to that, but it was business and they would understand. For now, she looked forward to celebrating and drinking with her girlfriends tonight, and most likely crashing on Allison's couch.

* * *

"Gizmo! Hey bud!"

Sarah was greeted by her three year old orange tabby cat when she arrived home. She kicked off her heels and sat on the floor to play with him for a few minutes. The trip home had taken over an hour, and next week it would undoubtedly take even longer once she started the new job, since the trains ran less often after midnight. She was dead set against driving in Manhattan, so she would deal with it for now. Gizmo purred as he climbed into her lap. She leaned down and gave him a kiss on his forehead.

She logged onto her computer and read the outpouring of well-wishes on her Facebook page. She "liked" all of them and responded to a few comments from some of her best friends and family. People were excited for her, and it made her feel good. She followed that up by checking the news on the presidential campaign. She was a staunch liberal and a fierce feminist. She wasn't thrilled about the state of American politics, and was not too excited about the democratic candidate.

As long as Trump doesn't win. She laughed at that notion.

She looked at the time. She could relax a bit and maybe take a nap before heading to her parents' house for dinner and then back to the city to meet Allison and the rest of the group in Brooklyn. She logged off the computer, took those business clothes off that she hated so much and tossed them on the floor in the closet, hoping it would be awhile before she had to dress like that again. She had always been a sneakers and jeans kind of woman. She went to the bathroom and weighed herself.

Shit.

She was tall—5'11" —with a medium frame, but 170 pounds was not where she wanted to be. Once she got settled in her new job, her next project would be shedding fifteen pounds. As she slipped into a tee shirt and sweat pants, she thought that maybe it was time to focus more on dating. Allison was getting married later in the year, and Sarah had been to numerous weddings since graduating from college. She was twenty-nine years old now and about to start a new career. Her love life was severely lacking and she'd never had a steady boyfriend.

Lose the weight first, then get into dating, she told herself as she yawned and nestled comfortably under the bed covers. Gizmo jumped up and joined her, curling up close. She laughed at herself. Her cat was currently the only man in her life and he was in bed with her.

Sarah McConnell slowly drifted to sleep, happy and content with life, and the direction it was going.

CHAPTER 2

THURSDAY AUGUST 25, 2016

Bruce Keller finished brushing his teeth, rinsed, and joined his wife of three years in bed. He wondered if enough time had passed to follow up on what he had asked her two nights ago. If she said yes—and he thought she would—nothing would ever be the same.

Marilyn was a blessing in every way. Bruce had been fifty-five years old when they met, and despite a very comfortable life after an unspeakable tragedy he'd experienced as a child, true love was the only thing missing and she complimented him perfectly. She was ten years younger than him, but despite their age difference she was the one woman who understood him.

"So, have you given any more thought to what we talked about?" Bruce asked his wife.

"Yes. And I'm in. I'm with you, one hundred percent."

Bruce let out a deep exhale.

"Good. I knew you would be. We already have everything we've ever wanted. So, we'll make sure everything is perfect, in case we don't get away with it. We'll start planning it tomorrow."

"Well, I thought of something else, actually," Marilyn replied.

"What's that?"

"First of all, we *are* going to get away with it. But I also think we could make money off this. *A lot* of money."

The number of people in the United States who are aroused by unusual and deviant sexual fantasies is much higher than the average person would guess. Most people are completely unaware of this and many others would rather choose not to believe it. With the explosion of the Internet came message boards and websites that cater to people with some of these interests. Some of the websites involve dark and violent fantasies and it was on one of those sites where Bruce and a female user began messaging each other about theirs. As it turned out, both had fantasies about committing brutal acts of violence on women.

That female user was now lying next to him in bed. Soon after they'd met online, they decided to meet in real life, so he had driven down to Bedford, Virginia where she lived and worked as a cashier at Walmart. They clicked in every way, and they fell in love instantly. Neither had any immediate family still living. Marilyn did not have any siblings and both of her parents had passed away from age.

Bruce was also an only child, and his parents had been killed in a boating accident when he was ten years old. He was left with a nice inheritance, however. His father had owned a very successful furniture company, and his father's best friend raised the orphaned young boy with his own family and took control of the company, prepared to hand it over to Bruce when he was ready. Once Bruce earned his MBA at New York University, he stepped in and took over as president. Through all of that, he harbored atypical sexual fantasies. It was something he'd kept hidden out of fear of being shamed and ridiculed. At the time, he had no idea how many people had similar thoughts. As he got older, his fantasies became more detailed and more violent.

Bruce eventually moved back into his family home, a 14,000 square foot, two-story house in the Hudson Valley, about two hours north of New York City. It was private and luxurious, secluded and peaceful, with many guest rooms and a large walkout basement with access to a spacious back yard surrounded by trees. The nearest neighbor was just over a half mile away. He enjoyed the tranquility.

Bruce drove down to Virginia for one weekend every month from March through December, 2012. He pampered Marilyn and treated her like a princess. They also fucked like wild animals, sometimes incorporating a few of her sex toys. With the arrival of the new year, they decided there was no better time to start their new life together. Marilyn moved up to New York to live with Bruce and soon after they got married. It was a small ceremony attended by some of Bruce's friends and employees, all of whom applauded when the bride and groom cut the wedding cake together. None of the guests knew of the violent sexual fantasies harbored by the newly married couple. It was a secret they kept from everyone outside of their online world.

They each kept their accounts active on the dark fetish website, and continued to communicate with people who had similar desires. In the bedroom, Bruce and Marilyn enjoyed role-playing abduction scenes and they used ideas from other members of the website to provide more variety. Eventually, that wore thin because Marilyn didn't particularly like being tied up. They were happy, but there was something missing and they both knew exactly what it was.

Bruce had finally brought it up two days ago, and now, while they lay in bed together, they agreed to plan and carry out a real life kidnapping.

Bruce's curiosity was piqued by his wife's suggestion. "What do you have in mind? We already have plenty of money."

Marilyn turned to face her husband.

"I know, but I've spent the last two days thinking about it. If we're really going to do this, we should do it as some kind of an event. We could film it and sell the video, or we could even have people come over and participate with us. We have the venue, we'd provide the victim, and we would charge people if they wanted to come."

"I appreciate your forward thinking," Bruce chuckled, "but it's already risky enough if it's just the two of us—"

Marilyn cut him off.

"I'm not too concerned about the actual kidnapping. We'd take our time and really make sure we cover all the risks. You don't think we could find a handful of people on the website who would want to participate in raping and torturing a girl?"

"I'm sure there would be, but it's really not worth it to me. I think you're a little too optimistic here. Yes, we'd plan it carefully. But there are still no guarantees even if it's just us. And you want to bring in people from the Internet we've never even met?"

"Look, just think about it. We have a lot of space here, and there are a lot of people on that website we've both communicated with who have very similar interests. The two of us connected, Bruce. And we're both willing to go through with a real plan. There are definitely others. Listen, there is still a lot to do before we get to that point. We need to figure out where we would keep the girl. We need to actually *pick* a girl. Then we need to watch -"

"Yes, there is a lot to do. We'll start brainstorming and come up with a list of things we need to buy tomorrow. As far as the girl and her captivity, it has to be the basement, don't you think?"

"Definitely. I had the same thoughts," Marilyn answered.

"The basement will need a lot of work. There's enough for us to do without worrying about putting on a show for people we don't know and can't trust. Some of them could be undercover cops."

Marilyn was frustrated.

"You don't think I know that? I wouldn't have brought this up if I hadn't done a little bit of research. Listen, just sleep on it. I have some ideas that we'll talk about later. This is going to sound crazy, but I had nothing before I met you. I lived in a small town down south, I had a shit job, no family, and that website brought me to you. Now I have everything with you. Providing an opportunity for others to act out their fantasies would be my crazy way of paying it forward."

Bruce shook his head.

Marilyn continued, "Like I said. I have some ideas. I've done some research. There are things we can do to skirt law enforcement. Just hear me out tomorrow, okay? Have an open mind."

"Please, humor me and give me *something*. Is my wife a tech whiz and I don't know about it?"

They each laughed.

"We'll have to find a way to vet people obviously, but I've looked into the dark web. There's special software that keeps IP addresses hidden, and all communication is encrypted. We'll create our own website, or forum, or whatever and pass it along to the people we know on the site where we met. It won't show up on search engines. Everything is hidden. If they are serious, they'll install the software and we'll take it from there. We'll get the people who are serious, and we'll get people who will pay," Marilyn said.

"You've been thinking about this before I even brought it up, haven't you?"

"Of course. We both knew eventually we'd want to do it for real."

Bruce leaned in and kissed his wife on the lips.

"You're the best thing that ever happened to me. To hell with the money, the house, all of it. You are everything, and we're going to stick together through this, no matter what."

He paused and looked sternly into her eyes. "You are absolutely sure, right?"

"Absolutely sure."

"Okay then. I want to look into some of this dark web stuff myself. I'll check it out at work tomorrow, and when I get home we'll talk about it and start to come up with a list of what we need, precautions we need to take, all of that. A real action plan. Any idea on a victim?"

"Not really anyone specific," Marilyn said. "Someone low risk. A stripper, a prostitute. Someone who wouldn't be missed right away."

"Right. Well, there are plenty to pick from out there."

* * *

Marilyn fell asleep first. Bruce lay next to her in bed awake with all kinds of thoughts rushing through his mind. He pictured the basement after it was converted. He imagined a woman restrained and completely at his mercy. He would be free to do anything he wanted to her. He imagined her screaming and then realized he'd have to research soundproofing. They didn't have neighbors nearby, but it would be wise to take extra precautions.

Actually, I'd want to rape her first. One of the guest rooms could be hooked up to accommodate that.

They would take every possible safety measure to avoid getting caught. He thought about body disposal for a second, then he came back to the image of the basement. He saw a table right in the middle of the room, along with handcuffs, ropes, all types of sharp metal instruments, and some kind of pulley system to hoist her up.

A fucking blow torch. Holy shit this is going to be good.

Cash payments whenever possible.

Then he thought about the victim and what she might look like. He had no idea who it would be, but she was out there right now, probably sleeping, dreaming, and totally unaware that their worlds would one day collide.

He knew that whoever was selected wasn't going to deserve it, but he had no problem justifying it. He'd suffered a terrible tragedy as a young kid. The universe owed him one, and he knew that he and his wife would be prudent and patient. They would capture the perfect girl.

CHAPTER 3

IT DIDN'T TAKE LONG FOR BRUCE to get on board with Marilyn's idea. His concerns were greatly alleviated once he did his own research, and after two weeks they were ready to start recruiting potential clients. The first couple of messages to users on the dark fetish site did not yield any positive results. Each user expressed their interest to keep all communication on that website; they didn't want to mess around with the dark web.

Marilyn knew someone who she thought would be in though, so on her third try, with Bruce sitting next to her, "SadisticMistress34" sent a message to "Torturer47", a user who she'd been communicating with for several years, sharing their violent sexual fantasies:

"Hey, I want to talk to you about something, but it's private and it would have to be off this site. Are you familiar at all with the dark web? Check out the link below and follow the directions. You have to install some software, but it's really simple. Let me know if you are interested and I'll give you more information."

In ten minutes, she received a reply:

"Sure, I am actually quite familiar with the dark web and communicating through encrypted message boards. Let me get set up. Are you online now?"

"I guarantee this guy will be in with us," Marilyn said to Bruce as she typed her response:

"Terrific. I will log in now. When you're on, look for me under the same user name and send me a message. See you soon."

* * *

Bruce and Marilyn made up a preliminary list with some of the items they would want to purchase and they'd add and subtract as they saw fit. The items were listed into different categories based on when they would be used:

ABDUCTION
CAPTIVITY/RAPE/TORTURE
CLEAN UP AND BODY DISPOSAL

They already had nylon rope and duct tape from their sexual role-plays. Many of the other items could be purchased at any Home Depot. They would just go to different stores, and would always pay cash.

Six days after their mutual agreement to actually kidnap a woman, Marilyn ventured into New York City and shopped at a sex store. She bought two sets of handcuffs, two sets of ankle cuffs, and a few of the largest ball gags she could find. That would suffice for now. On another day, she'd go to another sex shop and buy some more items.

It's a marathon, not a sprint.

They decided to keep everything they bought in a closet in the basement, and with time, they would have a frightening arsenal built up. There was still a lot to do to prepare the basement and the rest of the house. They were in no rush to carry this plan out. They would be patient, extremely careful, and for that they would be rewarded. Although they would hold off on picking out their victim until the house was set up, every time they were out they would spot a woman they thought would be perfect.

Bruce did have someone specific in mind. Leigh-Anne, the receptionist in his office was thirty-three years old with a great body. She had a girl-next-door look with stunning, gorgeous hazel eyes and a bubbly personality. She was married with two kids, but that wouldn't be a problem. Two days earlier, he had watched her from his office as she walked from her desk to the copy machine. He imagined a set of handcuffs on her slender wrists. He imagined cramming a ball gag into her mouth and restraining her for unspeakable acts of horror. He started to get hard. Leigh-Anne smiled at him as she passed his office on the way back to her desk.

It can't be someone that we know.

That was a hard line that Bruce and Marilyn discussed. Although doing someone he knew like Leigh-Anne had its advantages—she was a very outgoing and trusting person, he knew her schedule, and there could be a myriad of ways to get her into their house—law enforcement would likely question everyone who had contact with her once she went missing. It would be more prudent to kidnap a woman who they didn't have any ties to.

* * *

Marilyn and Bruce got the direct message from "Torturer47" fifteen minutes later and for the first time they were communicating on a completely secured medium with their IP addresses hidden, and their text encrypted:

Torturer47: Hello?

SadisticMistress34: Hi there, thanks for finding me!

Torturer47: No problem. I must say you've piqued my interest by setting this up.

SadisticMistress34: I should say that my husband is here next to me. His username on the site is BK290. You've spoken in the past, yes?

Torturer47: Yes of course. I had no idea you two were married. Way to keep a secret. So, what's up?

SadisticMistress34: First of all we are still pretty new to this corner of the net. I assume you know that everything here is encrypted and undetectable?

Torturer47: Yes I've actually been on several similar forums and I have seen all sorts of fucked up things.

SadisticMistress34: Great. Well you know the topics we've talked about. My husband and I are really going to do it. We're still in the very early stages of planning and we have a lot of work to do, but we're going to plan it well and we're going to do it for real. We're looking for others who might be interested in participating.

Torturer47: You guys sure, right? I anticipate that you've discussed this at length and you are aware of the amount of work that would go into carrying this out. If it's for real and it happens, I'd definitely be interested. Any timetable?

SadisticMistress34: Yes we are fully aware of the work and the risks involved. As for the timetable . . . not exactly. All we know for sure is that we'll do it here, at our home. We're in upstate NY and we need to get our place ready first. What we want to do is have it as some kind of event and charge people if they want to come and participate. Obviously we'd charge quite a lot for something of this nature, and while we are setting the place up we want to find people who might be interested, ones we can trust.

Torturer47: I like that idea. It makes sense. You could even film it and sell the video on the black market. There are ways to make money, for sure. Like I said, I've been on these sites for a while, and I can tell you that there would absolutely be people interested. I am not sure what you'd be planning to charge, but I know that I would be able to cover it, and I can think of others who could as well. There are so many people with violent desires but it's impossible to act upon them without risking getting caught, and if given a chance they would definitely want to do it.

SadisticMistress34: I'm glad I reached out to you then. By the way, my real name is Marilyn, and my husband is Bruce. We're up in the Hudson Valley, a couple of hours north of Manhattan. Are you anywhere around us?

Torturer47: Nice to formerly meet (as "formal" as this can be at this point). My name is Bill. I'm a sociology professor at Penn State, so not terribly far from you. I mention my profession, wondering if you've picked a victim out yet? If not, I have the pick of the litter here on campus. 18-22 year olds, sorority girls, really a lot to choose from.

SadisticMistress34: I'm sure you do, but we want to stay away from anyone who can be connected to us, you, or anyone else involved. Just much safer that way. We want to leave as few leads as possible.

Torturer47: There is one that really sticks out. She'd be ideal, but I completely get it and it makes sense. Listen, why don't I reach out to some of the people I know? I know a couple of ex-military guys who could help with the actual abduction. I am not sure of your ages, but I certainly couldn't pull it off by myself. Sadly, father time has caught up to me a bit.

SadisticMistress34: We consider ourselves middle aged, haha. But anything you could do to spread the word would be just great! The more people we have, the more ideas, the safer it would be for all of us. We want to make sure everyone can go on with their lives safely afterwards without any repercussions.

Torturer47: Of course. It could be done. I'd offer to be part of the planning, but I don't think I can travel up to New York due to work obligations. But I do think some of the people I know can help. Once it happens though, I will be there.

SadisticMistress34: You can trust them? We'd have to come up with some way of vetting everyone.

Torturer47: These guys I do trust. I've been communicating with them for years, just like you. They've done a lot of shady shit but they keep their mouths shut about it. I'm sure they know people they trust too, and we can keep it in that circle for now.

SadisticMistress34: All of this helps. Thanks a lot. We'll start getting our place ready in the meantime. This is all going to take a while before we even think about which girl to kidnap, but having a pool of potential customers would be great.

Torturer47: Sure, and people with different tastes too. You are comfortable using this messaging service, right?

SadisticMistress34: So far, so good.

Torturer47: Good. I'll tell my guys they can find you here. Good luck with everything, Marilyn and Bruce. And thank you for this idea and for thinking of reaching out to me. Life has been rather ordinary, and I never dreamt this possible. I really appreciate it.

* * *

"That went about as well as it could possibly go," Bruce said.

"I know! Jesus, I hope he comes through."

"It surprises me how many people would actually be willing to go through with something like this. People who want something they've never been able to have. And they obviously aren't mentally ill. Bill is a college professor. He knows guys who were in the military."

"You, my wonderful, handsome husband, own your own company!" She wrapped her arms around him, and he returned the embrace.

"You, my beautiful wife, are more dangerous than I ever thought."

They shared a laugh, and then Bruce continued: "Things are moving along very well. Let's just make sure we don't get too far ahead of ourselves. And we do need to come up with a way to figure out whether people are serious about participating. I don't want to plan this whole thing and then have people getting cold feet, or worse, ratting us out. You were one-hundred percent right. This will make us money."

"And worst case scenario, if people do back out, we'll have more time with her for ourselves," Marilyn said.

"That's true. I do have a feeling this is going to spread like wildfire and we'll see how Bill does out there."

"Yes, give him some time to get back to us. I'm going to head back to the city for more sex store shopping. Do you need anything while I'm out? I can pick up some dinner on my way back. How about fried chicken?"

"Sounds great. Have a good time and be careful."

When Marilyn left, Bruce took another look at the list. He scribbled "drain system?" into the cleanup/body disposal category. Multiple drains on the basement floor would be ideal when it came time to hose off all the blood spilled from their victim. He'd have to talk to a plumbing contractor about that.

CHAPTER 4

FRIDAY NOVEMBER 4, 2016

Here goes nothing, Sarah said to herself.

She hated the idea of online dating but her friends talked her into it. They told her it was the way people meet and hook up in this day and age.

I'm sure not going to pay to go on a date though.

Late Friday morning, before her final shift of her second week at the animal hospital, Sarah caved and created a dating profile on OKCupid.

SarahMCC89

29 / F / Straight / Single
Long Island, NY

Ethnicity: White
Height: 5'11"
Body Type: About Average
Diet: Mostly Anything
Smokes: No
Drinks: Socially
Drugs: Never
Religion: Catholic and somewhat serious about it
Politics: Very liberal but not too serious about it
Sign: Aries
Education: Graduated with Doctorate
Job: Veterinary
Income: Rather not say
Offspring: Wants children
Pets: Cat(s) and they live at home
Speaks: English

My self-summary:
Animal lover, food lover, people lover in that order. Down to earth, lifelong New Yorker with a sense of humor looking to meet

Mr. Right. Looking for serious relationships only, not casual hookups.

What I'm doing with my life:
Just started a new job as a chief veterinarian working the night shift at an animal hospital. The hours are rough, but it's fun. I promise, I'll spare you the details but you'll hear all about my cat :)

I'm really good at:
Unintentionally making a fool out of myself. Sticking my foot in my mouth, etc etc.

The first things people usually notice about me:
I'm pretty tall. It's easy to spot me. Despite my height, I never played basketball. Just to get that out of the way because I've been asked that a lot. In fact, I am the least athletic person you'll ever meet but I do enjoy jogging from time to time.

Favorite books, movies, shows, music, and food:
Books: All of the Harry Potter stuff. Anything sci-fi really. I'm kind of a nerd. I'll expand on this list at some point.

Movies: See above, and all of the Star Wars movies! Also love comedies. Oh and I've never seen the Godfather.

Shows: I loved LOST. These days I'm into The Walking Dead, The Daily Show, The Mindy Project, and a few more. I'll get back to this actually

Music: Mostly 90s music, but I'll go see anything live. I LOVE concerts and music festivals.

Food: Not very picky. I love cheese and Mexican food. I'm Irish so bonus points if you can make a mean corned beef and cabbage :)

The six things I could never do without:
Hmmmm, my phone, flip flops during the summer, friends, family, chap stick, and cheeeeeese. Not necessarily in that order.

I spend a lot of time thinking about:
Why I refuse to learn how to drive in New York City. I mean, it's a serious phobia.

On a typical Friday night I am:
At work! Until midnight, then it all depends on my friends, and YOU!

The most private thing I'm willing to admit:
I'm not very much into politics, but I consider myself very liberal. I believe in feminism and equal rights. I believe in a woman's right to choose. I believe in gay marriage. I can enjoy the company of someone on the other end of the spectrum, but if you're hardcore into politics and think that people on the left are morons/evil, then we wouldn't work out.

I'm looking for:
Guys who like girls
Ages 29-35
Located within 20 miles of Long Island, NY
Long-term dating

You should message me if:
If and only if you are looking for something serious. I like to joke around and have fun, I have great friends and a career that I am very happy with. There is just one thing missing, and I was hesitant to resort to online dating but I am giving it a shot. Not to be picky, but please at least have graduated from college and have a job. Also, please don't live with your parents. I want a strong, independent man. I want the walks on the beach, the nights out, cuddling on the couch and watching movies on rainy days, the whole thing.

So if that's you, say hello! :)

She uploaded some pictures of herself from her Facebook page and just like that, Sarah McConnell was in the online dating market.

Must be a cold day in Hell, she thought.

She hopped in the shower and then got dressed. She worked in a very relaxed office, and she could wear comfortable jeans and sneakers every day. She had her own white lab coat with "Dr. Sarah McConnell" stitched in script over her left breast. It was a light appointment day for her, and she hoped it would stay that way. As much as she wanted to help people and their pets, it still broke her heart to see animals that were sick and hurting.

She drove the ten minutes to the Long Island Rail Road station. She didn't want to pay for parking, so she always parked on one of the side streets, which was an extra three to five minute walk to the station. As long as the train was on time, her commute to work, in total, was about an hour and fifteen minutes.

Two-thirty p.m. wasn't a busy time to travel, and as usual, she was able to find a seat. She settled in and texted Allison:

"So, I did it. I'm on OKCupid lololol"

"OMG!! Sarah! Finally!"

"Lol, yeah we'll see. I'm still so skeptical but whatev."

"You're a total babe. You NEED to meet someone. I'm tired of hanging out with you. What are u doing after work?"

They made plans to meet at a bar on the Upper East Side close to the animal hospital. Sarah spent the rest of the commute doing some people-watching and catching up on social media. She hoped for a nice easy day at work, and afterwards a few Blue Moons with her best friend.

* * *

On the thirty-second floor of a Midtown Manhattan skyscraper, Jennifer Miller was getting ready for a first meeting with a new client. At twenty-seven years old and with just two years in the firm, she already had a reputation for being a first-class straight shooter and not sugarcoating anything with her clients. Her career as a financial planner was off to a great start.

She looked at the time. She had twenty minutes before the 3:30 meeting. She typically worked very long hours, but she was leaving work early today to rest up for her very first marathon tomorrow. It was a thirteen-mile run that she thought would be a breeze. She was building up for her ultimate goal of finishing the New York City Marathon next November.

Jennifer had excelled at both academics and athletics throughout her life. She had graduated from the University of Connecticut as a dean's list student with a degree in finance while also competing on the swimming and diving team. She then earned her MBA from the same university.

Other than her time in Connecticut, Jennifer was a lifelong New Yorker. Her parents lived in Brooklyn where she'd been born and raised. After college, the Manhattan financial firm hired Jennifer and as soon as she had enough money saved, she moved out of the Brooklyn home and rented a single-family house in Queens with an adjacent garage. She didn't have a car, but it was convenient when her parents came to visit. She had plenty of friends from high school and college who she kept in touch with, but she lived alone. She liked the serenity that came with living by herself and doing her own thing whenever she wanted without having to worry about disturbing a roommate.

She had a passion for three things: Success that came with hard work, everything to do with money, and physical fitness. She was in peak physical shape and very proud of her well-toned body. She was single, but not stressing out about meeting someone. For now, her priority was her career and making good investments with the money that came with it.

As Jennifer was reviewing the questionnaire her new client had sent in last week, her office phone beeped.

"Yes?"

"Your 3:30 is here," the receptionist said.

"Okay, he can have a seat. I'll be out in a minute to meet him."

He was fifteen minutes early. One thing that surprised her about her job was the number of people who showed up late to appointments. She never understood how they could say they were serious about saving for their future, but couldn't be bothered to show up on time. It always rubbed her the wrong way.

The other thing that incensed her was when new potential clients failed to bring all of the paperwork that she asked for. She wanted to help people, but she couldn't do it without their full financial picture.

It's their money, not mine.

"Hi, Mr. Harris?" Jennifer extended her hand to greet the well-dressed gentleman waiting in the reception area.

"Yes," Pat Harris replied, his eyes lingering a bit too long on her legs. She was used to it. Her legs were like magnets, it seemed, drawing much attention from both men *and* women.

"Jennifer Miller. Very nice to meet you. Why don't you take a walk with me to my office and we'll get started. Do you need anything? Water? Coffee?"

"No, I'm good, thank you."

He was properly dressed and had a briefcase with him, which was promising. He looked like he had it all together, so she hoped the meeting would go smoothly. While they made small talk in the hallway on the way to her office, she noticed him taking another peek at her legs.

"Why don't you have a seat right here. I'll pull out your questionnaire and we'll get started. Just one thing, Mr. Harris. I am very forward with people and I don't *ever* sweeten a situation if there is no sugar around. I never intend to come off as harsh, but I think blunt and honest feedback is most helpful for my clients. That being said, I'm confident that we'll get to a place of financial security that makes us both very happy. So, shall we?"

"Yes, that sounds great and I do appreciate honest feedback. My kids are still very young but you hear on all those commercials that it's never too early to start saving. All I care about is their college education."

"Definitely. And how old are your children?"

"Seven and five."

"Okay, and you are an electrician. May I look at what you've brought? Tax returns, bank statements, all of that good stuff."

"Sure, just a sec," Pat said as he opened his briefcase. "You asked for a lot, but I think I have everything here."

"Okay, wonderful. And yes, I know it's a lot but it really helps to give me an accurate picture," she said as he handed her a file folder loaded with paperwork.

She continued, "We won't get too much into the nitty-gritty today but eventually we'll get deep into money management; investment strategies, retirement strategies. I know your only concern is your kids' college, but for example, money you put in a retirement account will earn interest and can be withdrawn when you're fifty-nine and a half. And with just some quick math, it looks like you'll be there by that time."

Hope he doesn't take offense to that, but he did have kids a little later than usual.

"Yes, I did have kids somewhat late in life, but I just want to make sure they are taken care of."

At least we're on the same wavelength, she thought to herself.

"Definitely. And we'll see what we can do about that. Off the bat, one thing for sure is that you need to open an IRA and you need to contribute every year. That's just the start, but let me look at everything. I'm not going to do much talking, but I'll probably be scribbling notes down like a maniac. You can use your phone, or do whatever you like in the meantime."

* * *

"Have a good weekend Lisa," Jennifer said to the receptionist on her way out.

"You too, and good luck tomorrow. Kick ass!" she replied.

Jennifer typically stayed in the office until about seven o'clock, but since she'd left work two hours early today she would have to deal with one of her least favorite pastimes; rush hour on the New York City subway system. She walked down the concrete steps into the station, swiped her MetroCard, and descended even further onto the absolutely crowded platform. A man playing jazz on a trumpet sounded rather pleasant, but it was quickly drowned out by the arrival of her train. Of course, it was packed full, so she had to wait for the next one. In the meantime, she dropped a five-dollar bill in the trumpet player's tin can. He smiled and winked at her.

She made her way to the end of the platform, which would be closer to the station exit at her stop in Queens. Her heels clacked with each step, and nearly every man—and even some women—checked out her toned legs as she passed them.

For fuck's sake already.

She knew that she was attractive and that her business attire didn't hide that. She heard someone whistle in the distance, a catcall, but she ignored it. Luckily the next train rolled in quickly, and she was even able to get a seat.

On the walk home from the station in Queens, she stopped at a deli and ordered a grilled chicken salad. She was starting to get a headache, which was the last thing she wanted the night before her first marathon. She hoped that eating something and loading up on water would alleviate it.

She got home just after six o'clock, kicked off her heels and put the salad on the kitchen table. She took her phone out of her bag and saw that she had a missed call from her father.

"Hey Dad, sorry I missed the call. I was on the train. What's up?"

"Oh, nothing. I didn't know you were leaving work early. Are you all set for tomorrow? Excited?"

"Yeah, I'm all set. I have a little bit of a headache but I'm just going to have dinner and relax."

"Good luck, honey!" Jennifer heard her mother yell in the background.

"Mom says good luck in case you didn't hear that. Well, we'll let you go relax then. Let's get together though. We'll take you out for dinner tomorrow night if you don't have any plans."

"Okay, that sounds good. I'm not doing anything after."

"Good, we'll pick you up too. Good luck tomorrow, honey."

Jennifer changed into a tank top and athletic mesh shorts and settled in on her couch. She ate her salad, found a movie on Netflix, and was in bed at nine o'clock.

CHAPTER 5

TUESDAY DECEMBER 19, 2016

hh290: hello?

hh290: anyone there

SadisticMistress34: Yes, I'm sorry. We are here. Are you experienced?

hh290: yes and i was referred by greg

SadisticMistress34: Okay then, welcome aboard. We need to talk about a couple of things first.

hh290: yes go ahead i'm ready

SadisticMistress34: What is your proximity to the Hudson Valley? In upstate NY

hh290: i live in nyc. not far. and i can drive

SadisticMistress34: Great! You are only the second New Yorker out of thirteen so far.

hh290: ok what else? i am interested.

SadisticMistress34: A couple more things. We will try our best to give as advanced notice as possible before the event, but you have to understand that things can change quickly depending on whether the girl is successfully abducted on the day we shoot for. You also must know that we will be charging a lot of money for this. With that much money involved, would your personal life allow for flexibility and potential last minute changes?

hh290: yes it's fine i am retired. and money is not going to be an issue. who is the girl you picked?

SadisticMistress34: We haven't settled on one. There are a lot of possibilities. We are having a meeting with our team today to discuss that. We are also continuing to prep our home. Before we go on I just want to clearly say that what takes place here will not be easy to see. Even for the most hardened person. Whatever girl we choose will slowly and systematically suffer. It won't be for the faint of heart at all. Just so you are aware.

hh290: that's good that's what I want. the more she suffers the better

SadisticMistress34: Very well then. You're talking to the right people. Before I put you on the list, also know that we may be auctioning off the event. We have had more people interested than we thought and we won't be able to accommodate everyone. We'll have more information on that when we know. Also, before you're on the list you have to do something for us to prove you're serious.

hh290: ok what is it.

SadisticMistress34: Tomorrow I'll message you with the name of a woman in New York City. Someone who is somewhat prominent and easy to find. Likely a journalist/news anchor. Something like that. Whoever we name, we'll also provide the address where she works. You'll need to take a candid photo of her within a week, upload it, and send it to us here. It could be when she's on her way to or from work, whenever you want. Once you send it and we verify that it's her, you'll be on the list.

hh290: ok no problem. let me know who

SadisticMistress34: We will. This is our way of weeding out people who aren't serious. It's something that isn't difficult or risky, but it is a demonstration of your commitment. By the way, my name is Marilyn Keller, my husband is Bruce.

hh290: thank you for doing this. my name is howard helton

CHAPTER 6

TUESDAY DECEMBER 19, 2016

"Leigh-Anne! Get me that invoice from the printer please!"

To Bruce's employees and non-Internet friends, everything seemed normal. Leigh-Anne handed him the printout.

As usual, he complained about the incompetence of other companies they dealt with. "Why do I always have to be the one catching these fucking mistakes? Every fucking time! It never ends!" he yelled to no one in particular as he pounded his fist on his desk.

His employees were used to the rants, and it made them chuckle, especially today. The office was decorated for Christmas, Andy Williams was currently singing "It's the Most Wonderful Time of the Year", and Bruce's yelling seemed out of place and oddly funny. He always treated them fairly and with respect, and never gave anyone a hard time when they needed a day off. To a certain degree, employees were allowed to work their own hours, as long as they got the work done. He was a fair boss, and despite the latest tirade, a very nice man.

Or so they thought.

While Bruce was sending an e-mail to another associate, he got a text message from his wife.

"Confirmed. Still on for tonight. They will be here at 8. Very excited."

"Great. See you later."

"Any ideas for food?"

"You'll have to figure it out. Sorry. In the middle of a shitstorm here. They're probably burgers and beers kind of guys."

"Okay, no problem. Take it easy. Big night tonight."

This was a big step toward the main event. Word got around the dark web rather quickly, and soon people up and down the east coast were interested in more information. The two ex-military men mentioned by Bill, the Penn State college professor, ending up panning out and they recruited two more people themselves. Tonight, those four men were driving to Bruce and Marilyn's house to meet for the first time, to brainstorm and discuss the plan to realize their collective darkest desires at the expense of an innocent victim.

Those four, they claimed in encrypted messages, would be interested in handling the kidnapping if they were paid well for it. They had each taken a candid photo of their assigned woman in New Jersey, so they were in. Their payout for carrying out a successful abduction would be negotiated tonight.

At times, it was difficult for Bruce to balance his duties as president of a successful company with planning the event. He was careful to maintain his normal demeanor in public, and was certain no one noticed any changes in his behavior.

It was a challenge to hold his anticipation in. He and Marilyn were doing an admirable job staying in the present and being careful about everything. Maybe, after tonight, plans could be expedited.

Don't get ahead of yourself. Keep things slow. It will work out.

* * *

Just after 8 p.m., while Bruce and Marilyn waited outside, a car with four men pulled onto the property. The couple stood and Bruce waved the driver towards the garage, where they met them inside.

The smallest of the four was just over six feet tall. The tallest stood six and a half feet. They were all white, appeared to be in their thirties, and they were incredibly muscular and looked very humorless and intimidating.

"Guys, welcome. I'm Bruce, this is my wife Marilyn."

"Great to be here," the apparent leader of the group said as he extended his hand. "I'm Darryl, this is Tom, Hank and Willie."

"Our pleasure, guys."

Everyone shook hands and followed Bruce and Marilyn into the house.

"We have a fridge full of Bud Lights and some burgers ready to go on the grill. You guys hungry?"

"Yeah, we could eat, thanks a lot," Darryl said.

"Alright, why don't I show you around while my wife takes care of the burgers. That okay honey?"

"Yes, of course. And guys, grab a beer for the grand tour."

Each of the four men thanked her for the hospitality and cracked open a can of beer. Marilyn went to the back yard and got the grill going. Bruce led the way around the house.

"So, upstairs we don't really need to see. It's just our master bedroom and a couple of guest rooms. We'll talk soon about the best way to proceed, but since you guys are from out of town and there'll be a certain amount of work to be done before the girl is grabbed, you're always welcome to crash here."

"That's great, thanks, and much appreciated," Tom replied.

"Okay, so here on this floor," Bruce started as he led them down a hallway, "we picked out the biggest guest room, and this is where we'll hold her."

He opened the door. "We still have a lot to do in this room. But the bed will have restraints installed. Probably cuffs at each corner. I am also planning on installing a gambrel hoist right in the middle here. You guys are familiar with those, right?"

They answered in the affirmative by nodding their heads. Darryl said, "I use the Skin It Rite hoist for the deer I bag. Works for me."

"I definitely want to soundproof the room and I'm almost done soundproofing the basement. You might have noticed that we are somewhat secluded, but it couldn't hurt to take every precaution. Anyway, once the girl is here, it would take some time for the other customers to get here. As part of your payment—and just a small part—I'd offer you all the opportunity to rape her in here. However you see fit, but I'd ask that you do your best not to make any physical marks. I want to keep her as clean as possible for the other guests since they are paying a lot of money to be here. We'll clean her up real good before the actual event starts. Fuck her any way you want as long as you don't leave visible damage."

"Well, I think we'd all take you up on that offer," Darryl said.

"Damn straight," Willie added.

"Good. Now let's go see our pride and joy."

Bruce led them back down the hallway towards the basement and opened the door.

"I'll have some kind of locking mechanism installed, but no rush on that for now. Here's what's happening down here at the moment."

Installed on the ceiling and walls of the 1,500 square foot basement was heavy, flexible soundproofing material.

"This stuff will keep all of the screaming confined," Bruce said as he patted the material on one of the walls.

There were two spaces—one on a wall, and one on the ceiling right over the center of the room—that did not have the soundproofing material. In its place, at each spot, was a large mirror.

"She'll be able to see everything that's happening to her."

The men voiced their approval and Bruce talked about the amount of space, and how it would easily hold the number of people they anticipated coming, in addition to the four of them.

"I'm installing the gambrel hoist down here, and right in the middle of the room we'll have some kind of a table with either straps or cuffs at each corner. The table will be tiltable, so that she can be positioned flat on her back, or a little more vertical. Hence, the two mirrors."

He went on, "We have everything we need for restraining the girl and I still need to get the table and really good video equipment. The lighting is good down here. We definitely want to record the show down here. We might even be able to sell that for more money."

He continued, "The drains on the floor were just installed. That'll make the cleanup much easier when we're done with her. Water source and hose in the corner. We'll figure out the best way to dispose of the body. Let me show you some of the things we've bought so far."

Bruce opened the closet and wheeled out a table with a sheet covering its contents.

"What do you guys think about this array?"

He lifted the sheet, revealing a host of torture instruments for puncturing, cutting, burning, breaking, and electrocuting.

"*Holy shit,*" Darryl said slowly. He and his three partners checked out the tools, picking them up and excitedly voicing their endorsements. Bruce directed them back to the closet. Hanging on the side wall, neatly arranged on racks, were an assortment of metal cuffs, ropes, and gags.

"Man, you've got this placed hooked up," Hank said.

"This is pretty fucking incredible," Darryl added.

"Thanks, guys. I expect we'll have a group of people here with many different tastes. So, the more variety, the better. I want everyone to have their way with the girl however they want, with the goal of keeping her alive as long as possible. The worst thing for everyone would be for her to die right away. Well, worst for everyone but her. We'll come up with a system, maybe they go up one at a time and get ten minutes with her. Anyway, just thinking out loud. That's for Marilyn and me to figure out. Why don't we head upstairs and talk business?"

* * *

While they ate at the dinner table, Darryl and Tom talked at length about their military service overseas and the others sat rapt in attention. Then they all shared their stories about how they discovered the dark web, and Bruce remarked how fortunate they were, that the stars must have aligned perfectly for them to be together this night.

"Okay, you guys ready to talk money?" Bruce asked.

"Yeah, let's get that out of the way. I think we all have a figure in mind, but we want to hear what you are proposing first," Darryl said.

"Definitely," Marilyn said. "So, as of now, we have fourteen people who are interested in coming, and they all have money. There is no way we can have all fourteen people here, and we're *still* recruiting potential customers. I don't want to get too far ahead of ourselves, but if all goes well, a second event is a real possibility. But for the first one, we'd like to keep it around six to eight people."

Bruce interjected, "I mentioned getting it on video downstairs. That could net us some more money, but we wouldn't release the whole event. Just clips of about thirty seconds each, a teaser of sorts. That way, if there is another event, people will really want to pony up and experience it live in person."

Marilyn continued, "Right. We were also initially thinking about kidnapping someone like a prostitute, or a stripper, to minimize the risk. But that is so garden variety, just not that exciting at all. For more money, we could kidnap someone more accomplished. You know? Someone who is somebody in society. Someone who would be missed. We wouldn't ask you to do anything that would put you at greater risk if you aren't comfortable with it, but we would articulate that greater risk to the potential customers and ask for more money. We also think it would make the event more enjoyable for them. I mean, let's face it, anyone could kidnap and kill a prostitute. It happens all the time. We want to offer something special."

"What's the figure you have in mind?" Darryl asked. "Me and my guys can assess the risk factors of kidnapping any particular woman. Various elements would come into play of course, but what are you thinking?"

"We would probably hold an auction for entry into the event, with a minimum bid of $75,000. So, with eight winners, that would come out to $600,000 at a minimum. Since the kidnapping is absolutely critical to make this happen, we are going to offer you seventy-five percent of the total figure, including any money we make off the video afterwards," Marilyn said.

"We'd split that four ways, guys. What do you think?" Darryl asked his men.

"That's more than fair to me."

"I'm in."

"Let's do it."

"Great. Again, this doesn't happen without you guys, and you are taking all the initial risk, so we want to take care of you. On top of that, you'd get to fuck her too. But as far as the event goes, hands off her. You're welcome to watch, but the winners of the auction along with my wife and I get to do her and finish her off," Bruce said.

"We can live with that," Darryl said. "We'll take care of all the kidnapping details. We have access to a van, fake license plates, all of that. We each have firearms and stun guns. That being said, this will take a long time to plan. Once a target is selected, we'd want to watch her for at least a month. Maybe two. Do you guys have an idea of when you want this to happen?"

"Not as of yet," Bruce answered. "We've indicated online that the date is flexible, subject to change at the drop of a hat. We just want to have the right girl with as little risk as possible."

"And 'the right girl' means, like I said, someone accomplished, obviously very attractive. Would love a city girl, if possible," Marilyn added.

"It shouldn't be tough to spot suitable women. The hard thing would be narrowing it down, and will involve a lot of surveillance. We'd want to keep tabs on her all hours of the day, and then decide the best time for the abduction," Darryl said.

Tom, mostly silent through the evening, chimed in: "What we could do is come up with a pool of possibilities. The four of us could split up into teams of two, and identify possible targets in the city, or wherever. We can photograph them and send them to you, and you decide whether they'd be suitable. If you say yes, we stay with them for the day, find out where they work and live, get a good feel on whether we could get them, or whether it would be too risky. We'd look for certain things to determine the risk factor, like her living situation, her work situation, cameras in the area. All of that. Once we have a good number of possible targets, we'll narrow it down from there and ultimately decide on one. Ideally, like you said, a good, attractive woman with minimized risk."

"That sounds good to me. Honey?" Bruce turned to Marilyn.

"Yes, that makes sense and I think it will work," she said as she smiled.

"Okay then, we'll get started soon. We all need to coordinate time off from our jobs, but we should be good to start in a couple of weeks, after the New Year. The early sunset will make it easier to watch women without being spotted. And don't worry about materials needed for the kidnapping. We'll take care of all of that," Darryl said.

* * *

Once business was taken care of, they spent the rest of the evening drinking and talking more about their pasts. Even though they came from all different backgrounds, here they were in upstate New York, brought together through a common bond.

The lust and desire to snatch a young woman out of her everyday routine and brutally end her life.

CHAPTER 7

TUESDAY FEBRUARY 21, 2017

5 STARS—2/20/17

"Over the last month, my kitty suffered a steep decline and me and my husband made the incredibly difficult decision to put him down so that he wouldn't suffer anymore. Last week we brought him to Dr. McConnell. It was a very difficult day and I'll spare some of details, but I just wanted to say that Dr. McConnell and her staff are wonderful, professional people. Dr. McConnell in particular is so unbelievably compassionate and understanding. She let us take our time to say goodbye to our boy and she made us a clay paw print before he was put to sleep. I picked it up a couple of days later. Today, I received a hand-written condolence card from Dr. McConnell in the mail. These gestures are so above and beyond, and they were so helpful for us. I can't say enough good things about her."

Tara N.
-Manhattan, NY

Sarah got a little teary-eyed as she read the most recent five-star Yelp review. Euthanizing pets was the one thing that she hated about her job. "Mittens" was the third one since she'd started working at the Manhattan animal hospital. She always presented a strong outer shell, but afterwards she would lock herself in the office for a few minutes to cry in private. She knew that Tara would be a wreck for a few days and her heart ached for her.

Although it had only been four months, Sarah was already very well liked by her staff and her clients. She had twenty-two five-star reviews and three four-star reviews on Yelp. People cited her professionalism, her sense of humor, and the fact that she was very direct and incredibly easy to talk to. Sarah was a humble woman, but all of this felt good.

"Good evening, can I help you?"

"Yes, hi, we have a 6:30 with Dr. McConnell."

Sarah heard the exchange from her office and a minute later the receptionist knocked on her door, which was slightly ajar.

"Your 6:30 is here."

"Okay, thanks Christina. I'll be right out."

"He's doing the intake paperwork now. It'll be a few minutes."

Sarah clicked on the appointment details on her Microsoft Office calendar. This was the first visit to this hospital for "Marty", a six-year-old French bulldog. The reason stated is that he had a problem with his right eye. She waited five minutes for the paperwork to be completed, put on her white lab coat, and went to meet them.

"Hi, I'm Dr. McConnell. And who is this handsome little guy?" Sarah said as Marty jumped up on her. His right eye had a dark red spot in the pupil.

"This is Marty, and I'm John," the forty-something said, shaking her hand. They both laughed at Marty's overenthusiastic greeting.

"Okay, well, let's see if we can figure out what's going on with that eye!"

As she led the way to the exam room, she picked up the intake paperwork from the front desk and asked Veronica, one of the technicians, to join them in room number one. John spoke as he tried to keep Marty's excitement under control.

"He's still just regular Marty. He's not scratching his eye or rubbing his face in the ground or anything."

"That's very good. That was the first thing I was going to ask," Sarah said as she wrote on her notepad and reviewed the intake paperwork.

She continued, "So, no other issues going on, right? No coughing, vomiting, diarrhea."

"Nope, everything is all good but that eye is tough to look at."

"Did he have a bath recently? Sometimes the shampoo can get in the eye and cause some redness."

"No, he hasn't had a bath in a couple of weeks."

"Okay, when did you first notice the redness?" Sarah asked as she knelt to get a closer look.

"A couple of days ago. It's gotten more and more red. I looked up some stuff online and read that it could be basically nothing or something really serious so I wanted to bring him in."

"Yeah, definitely. I'm just going to take him to the back so Veronica can weigh him, and I'll get something to test his eye. We'll be right back. Is that okay, cutie pie? You want to come see the back?" Marty wagged his stubby tail and let out a short bark in agreement.

They returned to the exam room a few minutes later and Veronica asked John to help put Marty up on the exam table. Sarah said;

"What I'll do is put a couple of drops of a fluorescein dye in his eye, which will stick to any tiny little break in the cornea. Once I put the dye in, we'll turn off the lights and I'll shine this little ultraviolet light on his eye. If we see any dye, that means there's a scratch or a break in his cornea. So if you and Veronica can hold him down."

Sarah baby-talked Marty while she put the dye in. The examination showed exactly what she thought it would, and she diagnosed the dog with an eye ulcer. She handed John a bottle of eye drops and a tube of ointment.

"The eye drops are for any pain he might feel, and the ointment is to take care of the ulcer. He'll be fine. Just make sure he doesn't go in any bushes or anything that can poke his eye. If he takes a decent shot it could lead to more serious problems. I'd like to see him back here in a week for another dye test, if you can make it. You can come right in without an appointment. I'll take care of it with the front desk. No charge for next week."

She scratched Marty's ear and said, "Okay, handsome? Can I see you again next week?"

"I really appreciate that. Thanks so much, doctor. All things considered, this was pretty good news."

"Absolutely, but one more thing. He's a *little* bit overweight. He still has a decent figure but I'd like to see him a little bit lighter. Once they hit this age you're looking at all kinds of new potential problems. Diabetes, all that bad stuff. So just keep an eye on it, maybe a little less pizza."

Sarah and John shared a laugh.

"Will do. It's so tough to say 'no' sometimes."

"Oh, I know it. Trust me. Alright, so they'll take care of you at the front and we'll see you back here a week from today?"

"Definitely. Thanks again, doctor."

Sarah went back to her office to start a file on Marty. She didn't feel hypocritical anymore pointing out an animal's weight problem to its owner. This morning she was down to 160 pounds. After the holidays, she had signed up for a gym membership as well as Weight Watchers, and in just six weeks she'd already shed ten pounds. She felt so much more confident these days.

When she finished Marty's paperwork, it was time to eat. She never brought her own food because she couldn't cook. Every couple of weeks she would visit her parents and her mother would cook enough so that Sarah could take leftovers to work. But other than that, she enjoyed sampling the wide variety of eateries on the Upper East Side of Manhattan. Tonight she was in the mood for a turkey and Swiss sandwich from her favorite gourmet deli. It was usually packed this time of the night and it would be tough to get a seat, but if she couldn't get one she'd bring the food back to the office.

"I'm clear for the next hour. Going out for dinner," she said to the receptionist on her way out. "Any emergencies give me a call. I'll just be at the deli."

* * *

Darryl and Hank were on duty tonight.

They had a good parking spot and sat in Darryl's car listening to sports talk radio, making small talk and keeping an eye on the foot traffic. They were confident that they would find one tonight. It had been dark for three hours now and in this area of Manhattan they would never be noticed. People were either too busy with their heads in their phones, or concerned with getting from point A to point B as quickly as possible.

Tom and Willie made up the other team. Since Darryl and Tom were both ex-military, their tactical proficiency would work best if they were split up and partnered with the two other men. They figured it would minimize the risk.

Darryl and Hank had been working together for five weeks and they now knew exactly what they were looking for. In those five weeks they had found three that were approved and added to the list. Tom and Willie had found four. They wanted anywhere from ten to fifteen, then they would get together, discuss the risks associated with each girl, and make the final selection.

"Ten o'clock, crossing the street. What do you think?" Darryl asked.

Hank looked to the left and spotted the woman. She was tall with milky white skin and wavy black hair just past her shoulders. She walked with a purpose, wearing dark blue jeans and sneakers. The wind blew her hair into her face and she pulled it back with her hand. Dark nail polish—probably blue, but could be black—topped her fingernails.

"I'm on her," Hank said as he got out of the car with his phone and began to follow her. They knew each other well enough now to know exactly how to proceed. Hank shadowed her for two blocks. She walked into a crowded deli. He followed her in.

There was a fairly long line for sandwiches. While he pretended to browse around, he took his phone out and quickly snapped photos of her. She kept turning and looking at the seating area while she waited and he got good shots of her face. It looked like she was planning to stay and eat there.

Yeah, they'll probably like this one.

He continued to keep a close eye on her while he made himself a cup of coffee. She got her sandwich and headed towards the cash register. He timed it so that he was behind her on line. He was inches from her and he started to get an erection, wondering if she was going to be the one. This was always the hottest part, he knowing what they didn't, in part deciding her future, and she having no idea.

A table had just become available and she kept her eye on it. He watched carefully as she pulled her money out to try and spot her name on an ID or a credit card, but he couldn't get a close enough look. Her nail polish, as he accurately guessed from the car was dark blue. She paid for her sandwich and darted to the open table. She took her coat off. She was wearing a light blue sweater. Hank paid for his coffee as she sat down and pulled her phone out. She had half of her sandwich in one hand and her phone in the other, apparently scrolling through something.

Hank took a few more photos of her and then walked out. Darryl was waiting outside in the car, parked at a fire hydrant. Hank got in and sent the photos of the unsuspecting woman to Marilyn.

"Spotted in Manhattan," he typed.

They had a clear view of the deli entrance. If a cop made them move from the hydrant, Hank would get out and wait on foot but for now they were good. It only took two minutes for Hank to get a reply.

"Yes. Follow her."

CHAPTER 8

WRITTEN AT THE TOP OF A FRESH PAGE in Darryl's notebook was the number "4", with the date next to it. Beneath that, on separate lines, were the time and location she was first spotted, the time she left the deli, and the time she arrived at the animal hospital along with its address. That last entry was at 8:23 p.m. For now, they assumed that's where she worked.

Over the next few days, her every move would be written down in that notebook. When the order was given to follow someone, the other duo would also be involved. Eyes would be on her around the clock, and the two groups would take twelve-hour shifts. Tom and Willie were notified, and would provide relief in the morning.

It was now quarter to midnight and they still hadn't seen her leave the building. They were parked across the street and down the block with a clear view of the entrance. Hank got out and continued to watch the entrance while Darryl drove around the block to see if there were any other exits. He noted one emergency exit in the back of the building. They also looked for cameras. It was tough to tell in the dark, but there was apparently one affixed to a traffic light at the nearest intersection, and one across the street from the hospital outside of a pizza joint.

Finally, just after midnight, she walked out the front door.

"There she is. You good?" Hank asked as he put the small wireless earpiece in.

"A-firm brother," Darryl replied as he put his own earpiece in. He then scribbled the next entry on the next line:

12:07 am—Left hospital

Hank tailed her on foot. His job was to narrate the direction and to keep Darryl up to speed on her location so that he could stay as close as possible with the car.

"Good on audio?" Hank spoke softly as he followed her.

"10-4. I got you."

Eventually, a woman would be selected. The men would be paid extremely well, but until then they enjoyed this part of it. This woman they followed was a potential target simply because she decided to go to that deli on this night. A decision so simple, so elementary made by millions of people every single day, may end up costing this woman her life. The randomness of it all—it could have been one of so many others—amazed them. They had no idea where she was going to lead them, but they would learn all about her through constant and continuous surveillance. They already knew where she worked, but where did she live? Who were her friends? Was she fucking anyone? If not, why not?

It was a thrill.

"Still south on Second Avenue, approaching subway station on seventy-second. Stand by."

"Copy."

"She's entering the station at seventy-second. Going to lose you."

"10-4. I'll follow the train line in the car. Text me updates."

"Copy," Hank replied, then hung up the call. He followed her into the station, swiped his MetroCard in a few steps behind her and tailed her down the stairs to the downtown ramp.

"Downtown side," he texted to Darryl.

He stood about thirty feet from her on the platform. She had her phone out, scrolling the screen. He took his phone out as well and pretended to be preoccupied. Her attention was on her phone, only looking up for a moment when she saw a large rat scurrying across one of the tracks. It apparently didn't faze her.

The train pulled in moments later and he made sure to get in the same car. He texted Darryl each time they arrived at a station;

"Lex/63rd. Still on."

"57th still on"

"49th still on"

Darryl kept up aboveground and his partner had an eye on the target. His phone continued to buzz at each station.

"34th street she's off. Possible LIRR. Standby"

Hank was right. He followed her off the subway and into Penn Station on 34th Street. He didn't have a pass for the Long Island Rail Road, but he knew that he could purchase one on the train.

"At Penn. Will text you LIRR train line"

"10-4," Darryl texted back. While he waited, he jotted down her subway stops. The more information he could note, the better. His phone buzzed again.

"Port Jefferson line. 1:13 departure"

Darryl looked up the stops on the Port Jefferson line on his phone and started the drive to the first station in Long Island. He had a roughly twenty minute head start on the train. With very little traffic on the road, he was already out of Manhattan and well onto the Long Island Expressway when he got the next message from Hank.

"On train with her, departed on time. You on way to LI?"

"Yes"

On a weeknight at this time the train wasn't crowded at all. Hank sat seven rows behind her, but he could see the top of her head.

All right, honey. Where are you taking us?

He pulled out his wallet when the conductor entered the car.

"Tickets, please."

"Can I buy it from you? I don't have a pass and I was in a rush. I didn't have time to get one at Penn."

"Not a problem. Where are you headed?"

"All the way to the end. Port Jeff," was the only logical answer to give.

He paid his fare and kept his eye on the woman while the conductor punched a couple of holes in his ticket. He texted Darryl at the first three stops, letting him know that they were still on the train.

Darryl, well ahead of the train, waited at each of the stops. Finally, when the train pulled into the Mineola station, he received the text he was waiting for.

"Mineola, she's getting off"

"Got you I'm here. Call me"

Hank dialed him. It was just after 2 a.m. and the area was desolate. Darryl easily spotted her, and his partner trailed about sixty feet behind her.

"Good on audio?" Hank asked.

"Good. I have eyes on you too."

Hank communicated the route, and Darryl stayed behind in the car. She walked for five minutes, then turned onto a side street and took something out of her purse.

"Looks like she's getting into a car," Hank said when he spotted the car keys. "Dark blue Taurus. You with me?"

"Right behind you. I see her. Get in."

Hank got into the passenger's seat and they watched the woman get into her car. Hank took the notebook and jotted down the time, the make of the car, and the license plate number. They kept a safe distance as they followed her.

"Ten over the speed limit," Darryl said. "Not bad for a chick."

She made a left turn and slowed down. Ten minutes later she pulled into a spot in front of a small house and got out of the car. The block was very quiet, the houses were dark.

Hank wrote the next entry into the notebook; the exact time and the address of her house. Darryl called Tom to give him their current location while Hank texted Marilyn.

"Successfully followed target home, she will be watched for the next few days."

Tom and Willie would take over at 8 a.m. Everything was good to proceed.

* * *

"Hi, Gizmo! How's my little guy today?"

Sarah put her purse on the dining room table and played with her cat before taking her coat off. She sat on the floor and he climbed onto her lap.

"Hey, don't get too comfortable kiddo. Mommy's tired."

She picked him up and carried him into the bedroom, took her coat off and tossed it onto a chair. She was exhausted. She took off her sneakers and socks and sat in bed Indian-style while checking her e-mail on her phone. Nothing other than an iTunes receipt.

No news is good news.

She hadn't logged onto OKCupid in a while, so she decided to check it out. She had fourteen messages in her inbox, the majority of which were one or two words:

"Hey"

"Yo"

"What's up?"

There were a couple of longer ones, but nothing that impressed her. Obviously they hadn't bothered to read her profile, instead had just looked at her photographs.

What a waste of time.

She washed up and slipped into her pajamas, turned the lights off and went to bed. As usual Gizmo joined her. The covers were warm and cozy and she slowly drifted to sleep. Sarah McConnell was a daughter, a friend, a brilliant and well-loved veterinarian. Tonight, unbeknownst to her, she was also number four in Darryl's notebook.

CHAPTER 9

WEDNESDAY FEBRUARY 20, 2017

Bruce and Marilyn kept things well organized. Their "kidnap team" had collectively spotted and briefly surveilled eight women, and the couple had paper files on each one.

Marilyn had printed out pictures of the girls and paper-clipped her favorite photo to the front of their file. At this point, they didn't have much information on most of the targets other than home addresses, where they worked, or went to school. Whether they lived alone, were married, or had boyfriends. But they all fit Bruce and Marilyn's criteria. All eight were attractive and appeared to have successful lives.

This most recent target had amassed the most information by a landslide. The next morning Bruce called Willie, who was currently surveilling her.

"Did Darryl write down the address of her workplace?" he asked.

Willie found it in the notebook, and Bruce googled it. The animal hospital on the Upper East Side of Manhattan came up on top of the search results. He clicked the website link, and saw a tab that read "Our Team" at the top of the page. The girl from Mineola now had a name for her file.

That night, the two of them went through each file and discussed their favorite targets. They came to the last file on the girl from Mineola. Sarah McConnell. Clipped to the front was her photo from the animal hospital website. She was wearing a white lab coat, smiling, and holding a cat. Inside the file was a printout of her biography page from the website, pictures taken by the kidnap team, information on where she lived and where she worked. They found her Facebook page, and Marilyn printed out some of her favorite photos and added them to the file.

Quite a character. Definitely a life-of-the-party type, Marilyn had thought to herself while reviewing Sarah's Facebook photos.

Bruce and Marilyn agreed that she was the least attractive of the eight, but the fact that they already had so much information on her excited them. Marilyn took the printout of the biography page out of the file and read it again:

"Dr. Sarah McConnell grew up on Long Island. She received her undergraduate degree in animal science at Columbia University, and her DVM from Cornell. While at Cornell,

she participated in a prestigious national conference for veterinary students in Kansas City, Missouri. Dr. McConnell practiced on Long Island before joining our team in October of 2016. Outside of the clinic, Dr. McConnell enjoys the company of her cat Gizmo, concerts, and traveling."

Their research also led them to her stellar Yelp reviews.

"I just love her. I really do," Marilyn said.

"She's definitely in the running. She's not the prettiest one, but she makes up for it in other ways. She would definitely be missed," Bruce said.

"She's a *genius* too. Ivy League schools, a beautiful smile, and definitely quirky," Marilyn replied, citing a few of her Facebook posts.

"We'll see. Let's wait until the guys come up with a couple of more, then we'll have a meeting and talk it all out. They'll have their opinions on which ones will be easiest to kidnap. That's important. Don't get your heart set on Sarah, in case they decide that she would be too risky."

"Oh, don't be such a downer."

"I do like her too, though. A lot."

Marilyn's phone beeped. It was a photo message from Willie. He and Tom had spotted another possible target.

"My oh my, look at this one!" Marilyn said, showing the photos to Bruce.

The pictures were taken in a bar. The girl was tall, absolutely gorgeous, and wearing tight fitting clothes that revealed an impeccable body.

"Jesus, she is fucking *stunning*," Bruce said.

Marilyn replied to the text.

"Yes. Follow her."

* * *

"That guy over there is *totally* checking you out, and he's *definitely* hot."

"No, no, no. C'mon. It's us tonight. No guys!"

"Jennifer! He's so fucking sexy. He wants to talk to you!"

Jennifer was celebrating her twenty-eighth birthday with two of her best friends in a Brooklyn bar. She had just made eye contact with the guy sitting at the bar who was clearly into her. He *was* hot as hell but she wasn't there to pick up guys. She just wanted to have a fun night with the girls.

Danielle, her friend from UConn, took the decision out of her hands and made a beeline towards the guy. She took him by the hand and walked back with him.

"It's my friend Jennifer's birthday and you two need to talk," she said through slurred speech.

"Hi, I'm sorry," Jennifer said to him while smiling.

He was about six feet four, very muscular, and had a broad smile.

"It's okay. Can I buy you a birthday shot?"

"Sure. Jamo okay?"

"You got it. Jennifer, right? I *think* that's what your drunk friend said."

Jennifer laughed. "Yeah, Jennifer."

"Cool, I'm Jack. I'll be right back."

"So you're a poet, right?"

The two laughed and then he went to the bar, returning with two shots of Jameson. They toasted to her birthday, clinked glasses, tossed back the shots.

"Whoa, that one hit me," Jennifer said.

"Me too, kind of. I'm not much of a liquor guy, but it's all good."

The chemistry between them was unmistakable to her. She was glad that Danielle had taken it upon herself to play matchmaker. He bought two Miller Lites and they drank their beers as they made small talk and got to know each other. He mentioned that he'd been in the military and had done three tours in Afghanistan. After only ten minutes she knew she wanted to see him again.

"What do you do for a living, Jennifer?"

"I help people manage their money, help them make investments, that kind of stuff."

"Oh, so like a broker or something?"

"Financial advisor."

"Here in the city?"

Jennifer told him the name of her company, which he was very familiar with, since it was very well known. He asked her where her office building was, and she told him.

"So what do you do now?" she asked.

"I have a boring job. It's not that important. Hey, listen, I'm really sorry but I just noticed the time and I have to run. I have this thing I can't miss."

He put his half-empty glass of beer on a table. Jennifer's heart sunk. It had only been fifteen minutes and he suddenly wasn't interested anymore. He wouldn't even tell her about his job.

"I'm really sorry. I hope you enjoy the rest of your birthday though."

He's not even going to ask for my number?

"Thanks. Sorry you have to run. It was nice meeting you."

"*So* so nice to meet you Jennifer. It was a pleasure. Have a good night."

He kissed her on the cheek and walked out. Jennifer was absolutely dumbfounded. Her two friends sat at the bar and they were laughing. Jennifer went back to join them.

"Okay, so is like *Candid Camera* going to pop out from under the bar and say 'Ha ha gotcha'?"

Jennifer's two friends laughed hysterically. She chugged the rest of the beer from the glass.

"I need another fucking shot," she said.

* * *

"You all done in there, Casanova?" Tom asked.

"Fuck you, asshole," Willie responded.

The two of them laughed. Willie perfectly described the look on the woman's face when he bailed on her. He texted Marilyn that they would start on her in the morning.

"What's her name?" Tom asked.

"Jennifer."

Willie told Tom that she was a financial advisor, and filled him in on the location of her office building. It was just after 9 p.m. Tomorrow would be a long day for them, but hopefully a productive one. Jennifer, the beautiful birthday girl, was now number nine.

CHAPTER 10

SUNDAY APRIL 23, 2017

Eight months after Bruce and Marilyn first formed the plan to kidnap a woman, the final item was added to the basement. Though he wanted to use cash whenever possible, Bruce could only find this item on the Internet and was forced to put it on his credit card.

Early this Sunday morning, Marilyn heard the power drill going in the basement as she was brewing coffee, and took him a cup. Her husband was drilling into the new table in the middle of the room.

"Thanks, honey," Bruce said.

"Ah, now I see what you're doing. Eyebolts."

"Exactly."

The wood table was massive, 8 x 4 feet, with a tilting base. With the wheels locked in place, it couldn't be moved. Bruce took a sip of coffee, put his goggles back on and drilled the last of four eyebolts into the table, one in each corner.

"Then we just attach some cuffs or rope to each one," Bruce said.

"Wow. It's absolutely perfect."

Right above the bottom end of the table was a pulley and rope hoisting system. Attached to its hook was a spreader bar with leather cuffs at each end. Simple but effective. A similar hoist had been installed in the guest room, where the victim would be held captive until it was time for the event.

They also now had high-definition recording equipment stored in the closet of the basement. Many smaller purchases had been made over the last several months, but now, finally, they thought that they had everything ready to go.

"We should have the meeting with the guys soon and decide on a victim," Bruce said.

"You know, I was actually thinking of a dry run. Before we have the girl for the main event here. Maybe we should test some of this stuff out? Make sure it works?"

"I don't know. It makes sense but the guys already have their hands full. I can't ask them to do multiple women."

"Actually, I was online last night when you went to bed and I had a very intriguing conversation with someone about it. I still have it on the computer. Why don't you come up and read it for yourself, then let me know what you think."

Chris117112: Hey, I was referred to you by Ollie (Stalker666).

SadisticMistress34: And are you experienced?

Chris117112: Very much so. I am all in. Do you have a girl picked out yet?

SadisticMistress34: Not yet, but hopefully very soon. We are going to have a meeting soon to talk about that. Once we decide and we think we can get a date, we'll send out a message to everyone and include photos of her.

Chris117112: Sounds good. Out of curiosity how many people have expressed interest?

SadisticMistress34: You are number 36

Chris117112: Holy shit! Well maybe that number isn't all that high. But wow that's actually a lot of people.

SadisticMistress34: It is more than we thought for sure. Obviously we can't have all 36 people, so we are going to hold an auction for entry into the event. We'll have the info on that once we have a plan in place for kidnapping the girl. We're working on some other things though, like maybe recording it in pieces and selling it to the people who couldn't make it for the live show.

Chris117112: That would be awesome. I'd love to be there when it happens but if I can't it would be great to have the video. Hey maybe this is me trying to get into the event somehow . . . I'm not exactly loaded with the kind of money that you'd likely be asking for, but can I ask you something?

SadisticMistress34: First, where are you located? Are you anywhere in the northeast?

Chris117112: Yep, Steuben County NY.

SadisticMistress34: Oh great. We are in the Hudson Valley.

Chris117112: I just looked it up. It's about a four hour drive.

Wouldn't be a problem.

SadisticMistress34: What do you do for a living? By the way my name is Marilyn and my husband is Bruce.

Chris117112: I'm Chris. I'm a chef in a restaurant which kind of leads me to that question I was going to ask.

SadisticMistress34: Oh, what is it then?

Chris117112: Has anyone mentioned butchering and cooking the meat?

SadisticMistress34: Of what, the girl?

Chris117112: Sorry, yes. The girl you choose. After she is killed, there would be no reason to let the body go to waste. I live in deer hunting heaven, and I've butchered more deer than I can count. I ask because if people are interested in trying it out, I can butcher the carcass. It would be similar to a deer. I'd do it free of charge.

SadisicMistress34: Well, no one has mentioned that, but I could possibly run it by everyone. I do know that when I was on that dark fetish site, there were a lot of people into cannibalism.

Chris117112: There certainly are. I think it's one of those things that people are embarrassed to admit. Rape her up the ass? Hell yeah! Torture her slowly? Right on! Carve out a piece of her thigh and throw it on the grill? Now you're getting weird, haha.

SadisticMistress34: lol

Chris117112: Seriously though, for an event like this it wouldn't be weird at all. The only weird thing would be letting the body go to waste without anyone at least trying it. I could butcher the carcass, and I'd do it right. Meat is meat, whether it's from a pig, a deer, or a human female.

SadisticMistress34: It sounds interesting. You do make a valid point about wasting the body. We do need a method of body disposal, ha!

Chris117112: I'm telling you, it makes perfect sense. Would you run it by your husband/whatever crew you got there?

SadisticMistress34: I sure will.

Chris117112: Just one more thing really quickly, so I don't waste your time.

SadisticMistress34: Yes go ahead.

Chris117112: If I were going to do this, I'd need a decent amount of space and I'd have to be able to hang the carcass up by the ankles.

SadisticMistress34: Oh that would not be a problem. By the way, you do have to do something before you are officially added to the list. We have our little system of weeding people out so as not to waste OUR time.

Chris117112: Ok what's that?

SadisticMistress34: There's a news anchor, a woman who works for the local Steuben news station.

Bruce continued to read the conversation.

"He sent the photos of her in this morning. She must work nights," Marilyn said.

"Okay, so he's on the list then." Bruce took a deep breath and continued, "Cannibalism? You want to think about this?"

"Well, we're not into it, but what he said did make sense. There might be at least a couple of people who would want to do it. Why not? No one else will ever know except us, the guys, and the customers."

"Yeah, I guess. I wouldn't have a problem with it. You want to see if you can get him again?"

SadisticMistress34: Hey Chris, you there?

Chris117112: Hey good morning! Yes I'm here.

SadisticMistress34: Good, thanks for sending the photos. You're on the list! Congrats.

Chris117112: Awesome! Thanks. Hey I thought of something else by the way.

SadisticMistress34: Oh? What's that?

Chris117112: I have a niece who lives on Long Island, not far from the city. She's 18, about to graduate from high school. I've had this plan to kidnap and butcher her, but I'm not sure how to do it without getting caught. My place is too far away, too risky. I don't see her too often, and she wouldn't come up on her own. If we can get her to your place, I'd do her for you and you can try her. I do know her address.

SadisticMistress34: Bruce said he wants to see a picture of her. Do you have any?

Chris117112: Sure, one sec.

Chris117112: <jackie.jpg>

SadisticMistress34: Wow! She is gorgeous. Blond hair and look at those blue eyes! And what a body . . .

Chris117112: Isn't she? Her legs are to die for. She's a varsity soccer player. That's where the best meat is also. The legs and the rump. Anyway as I said, if you want to help me get her and I can use your place, this one is completely on the house. If you are happy with my work, then maybe we can talk about the event.

SadisticMistress34: I don't see any problem with that. We were thinking about doing a dry run before the event, so Jackie could be our guinea pig. Let's exchange phone numbers?

Chris117112: Sure, just one more condition though . . . about Jackie.

SadisticMistress34: What's that?

Chris117112: I don't want her to suffer. Sorry, I should have told you before I sent the picture. She is a really, really sweet girl and my sister and her husband will be devastated. They are all very close. Anyway, I do have feelings for her because she's family and she definitely doesn't deserve this, and especially doesn't deserve to suffer. I'd want to kill her quickly and as painlessly as possible before butchering the body.

SadisticMistress34: Okay that's no problem Chris. We understand. We're still interested though. Let's talk and figure out how to do this as soon as possible!

Chris117112: Great. What's your phone number?

* * *

Bruce answered his cell phone.

"Brucey boy, what's happening?"

"Hey, Darryl, how are you?"

"Very well, thanks. Are you happy with the possible selections?"

"Yes, we both are. Sorry we've been a little out of touch the last few days. We've been busy getting the place ready and we just finished this morning.

We'll be ready to have a sit down with you guys soon."

"Sure, just let me know when. Whatever you tell us, we'll make it work. We're basically ready to go. We just need to decide on a girl so we can plan the snatch."

"Very happy to hear that. Things are a little hectic here for the next week or so. Can you guys come up Saturday, May 6th? We'll have our girl picked out then."

"May 6th is good for me. I'll run it by the boys first but it should be fine."

"Thanks a lot, Darryl. If anything changes let me know. If not we'll touch base next week and confirm on Friday."

Everything was falling into place beautifully. The meeting with the kidnap team was set, and the house was fully equipped for the event. It was now time to focus on their newest project:

The abduction of Jackie Nixon.

❧

CHAPTER 11

FRIDAY APRIL 28, 2017

The alarm on Jackie's phone woke her up at six in the morning. She sat up in bed for a moment, rubbed her eyes and stretched. Her whole body was sore from working out the previous night. Senioritis had hit her like a ton of bricks, but the schoolwork down the stretch wasn't difficult. In fact, she'd coasted through four years at a Catholic school that had a reputation for a demanding and challenging curriculum. She'd scored a 1440 on the SAT and was a star player and captain on the school soccer team. She was rewarded with an athletic scholarship offer from the University of Pittsburgh, which she'd accepted.

At least it's Friday.

She turned the nightstand lamp on, made her bed and laid out her outfit for the day. The Catholic school offered very few options. Between the typical button-down shirt and the royal blue senior polo shirt, she chose the latter, along with a navy blue skirt and navy knee-high socks.

She quietly gathered what she needed for the bathroom. She was always the first one up during the week since her school was so far away and she had to take two buses. The Nixons were a middle-class family with only one car and her parents both worked close to home on Long Island. Jackie was very independent, and she'd insisted on taking the bus rather than have them getting up earlier to drive her.

It didn't take her long to get ready in the morning. She was a bit of a tomboy, but she knew that she was a looker. She was five-feet-seven inches tall with a well-toned body, big blue eyes, and long blonde hair. She had a ton of friends and a lot of guys at school had a crush on her. One of them would be her prom date in three weeks. He was a pitcher on the baseball team and was also Pittsburgh-bound in the fall. She kept it well hidden, but she liked him a lot and since they would be attending the same university, Jackie thought the two of them could possibly become an item.

We're probably going to hook up at prom and become official.

They'd have the summer together before going off to school. They were both athletes and college would be busy for both of them, so it made sense to have some time together before then.

This is the last thing I want to stress about. Snap out of it!

She got dressed and slipped on a pair of black leather flats. She checked the weather on her phone and decided that she didn't need a jacket today. With her hair still damp, she put it in a ponytail. She took her very light book bag and went downstairs to the kitchen.

"Hey, Daddy," she said to her father, who was brewing coffee in his pajamas.

"Good morning, sweetheart. Hey, when do we pick up the prom dress again?"

"It's *next* Saturday."

"Okay. I'll see ya later. Gotta go get my shower." He pecked her on the cheek and headed upstairs.

Jackie had time for a quick breakfast, so she toasted half of a bagel, spread cream cheese on it and wolfed it down with a glass of orange juice. She took her keys, threw her book bag over her shoulder and left the house.

It was a gorgeous Spring morning. The birds were chirping, something she hadn't noticed in a while because it had been raining nonstop for the past few weeks. She loved birds and their singing made her smile. A car horn beeping from close behind interrupted the moment. It beeped a few times.

Give it a rest, pervert.

The driver honked the horn again before pulling up on her left. She stepped up her pace, glanced at the beige minivan. A woman sat in the front passenger seat with the window down.

"Jackie!" a male voice familiar to her yelled from inside of the vehicle.

She peered in and saw the driver, her frown quickly turning into a glowing, sunny smile.

"Oh my God! Uncle Chris? Jesus, I thought you were some creeper."

Uncle Chris and the woman in the front seat laughed.

"Well, maybe that's up for debate," he said.

Jackie laughed and asked him what he was doing in town.

"I'm visiting your Mom and I'm going to show my friend around the city later. This is Marilyn. Marilyn, this is my niece, Jackie."

Jackie shook her hand.

"She didn't say anything to me! I wish I'd known you were coming."

"Yeah, it was a bit of a last minute thing. Listen why don't you hop in and I'll give you a lift to school?"

"Oh no, I'm totally fine. It's not much further to the bus stop."

"Oh stop it. It's no trouble. I insist. We can catch up a bit."

"Oh man, are you sure? I don't want to hold you up."

"Jackie, c'mon. It's been awhile! We'll see your Mom after I drop you off."

Marilyn opened the door and got out of the front seat.

"C'mon, the front seat is yours. I'll sit in the back," Marilyn said.

"Okay, thanks *so much,* guys."

* * *

The pictures don't do her justice. She is a bombshell, Marilyn thought to herself.

A few nights earlier Chris had packed his butcher kit and a travel bag, and made the long drive to Marilyn and Bruce's house in the Hudson Valley. The rear windows of the van were tinted and he had removed the back row of seats. They talked long into the night about Jackie and the plan to abduct her. Plan "A" sounded like it would work.

Bruce and Marilyn had already researched and bought the ingredients needed to synthesize their own liquid anesthetic, bleach and acetone, and cooked up a batch of chloroform. They also learned that it didn't work like it did in the movies. Five seconds of breathing it in wasn't enough to render the victim unconscious. It could take closer to two minutes before the person was totally out, and depending on the dosage of the solvent, some brain damage could result. For their purposes, that wasn't a concern. As long as the victim regained consciousness, fully awake and alert.

Marilyn had volunteered to be the test subject. Bruce poured a small amount into a cloth and put it over her nose. After about two minutes she waved her arms, signaling that she was feeling faint and on the edge of unconsciousness. They were satisfied with their product, and had enough to fill four twelve-ounce glass bottles, which were stored in the refrigerator.

Marilyn had one of those bottles with her now, and she cautiously took it out of her bag as she sat directly behind the unsuspecting blonde.

For the past two mornings, she and Chris had staked out Jackie, following her in Marilyn's car from the house to the bus stop. They identified an area along her route that didn't have any cameras. Getting her into the minivan shouldn't be difficult at all.

When Marilyn stepped out of the minivan, she eyed the young blonde from head to toe, sizing her up. She could not wait to see that 18-year-old naked body. She and Bruce were definitely all in.

Eating human flesh. There can't be many better than Jackie for trying it the first time.

Marilyn took the rag out and put it on her lap, catching bits of pieces of chat about school, soccer, her plans for the summer and the University of Pittsburgh. She was focused on their location and making sure that Jackie didn't use her cell phone. If she did, she would have to pounce earlier than they wanted to.

She loved the sound of Jackie's voice. She recalled moments ago shaking her hand and feeling her cool skin. She got wet between her legs, thinking about what they would do to her later.

This kid has no idea.

"Which way are you going?" Jackie asked her uncle.

"Oh shit, did I miss the turn?"

"Yeah, you had to make a right back there. No big deal."

They were getting very close to the predetermined location. Marilyn opened the glass bottle of chloroform and soaked the rag. Her heart raced. The moment she had been fantasizing about for decades was seconds away. Chris made the final turn onto a desolate dead-end street.

"Uncle Chris? Are you lost? I know it's been awhile since you've been here. Maybe I should slide over and drive," Jackie joked.

He ignored her. Checking his surrounding and deciding they were safe, he uttered the code phrase.

"So, do you feel like taking a trip?"

Before Jackie could answer, Marilyn reached around from the back and crammed the chloroform-soaked rag into her face, pinning her head to the headrest.

"Fucking breathe it in!" Marilyn yelled.

Assisted by built-up adrenaline that surged through her like wildfire, Marilyn had a good hard grip. The girl put up a decent fight though, squealing like a pig and flailing her arms, trying to strike Marilyn's face. Chris grabbed his niece's left arm and held it down. She screamed, she kicked her legs, and tried to fight free any way possible.

"You good back there?" Chris asked.

"Yeah, I got her. She'll go down any second now."

Chris made brief eye contact with his niece, saw absolute fear in her eyes. He looked away. Despite his desire to carry this through, he felt a tinge of remorse. She was family, and she undoubtedly would have had a very bright future.

It's okay. I know you don't understand, but it has to be done and it will be as painless as possible.

He looked down at her legs and when they stopped kicking, his eyes went up to her face. He watched her eyes roll up and her body go completely limp. Marilyn held the rag in place for ten more seconds after she fell unconscious, just to be sure, then tossed it to the back of the minivan. Jackie's comatose body slumped to the left, her mouth slightly open.

Chris rummaged through his niece's book bag, found her cell phone and removed the battery.

Meanwhile, Marilyn unbuckled Jackie's seat belt and dragged her to the back of the van. Once she was safely on the floor—out of public view—Chris shifted into drive and began the journey back to the Hudson Valley. He was careful to drive at speed limit and obey all traffic laws to avoid drawing attention from police, but the drive was already nerve-racking nonetheless.

Rush hour traffic soon. We'll be all right.

"Just make sure you keep her asleep, okay? The less time she's aware of what's happening, the better," Chris said.

"Oh, you're no fun!" Marilyn said from the back as she looked down at the victim. She ran her hands up underneath the polo shirt feeling her smooth, toned stomach and her firm breasts under her bra.

She closed her eyes and moaned. So far, it was better than she'd ever imagined it would be.

And we haven't even started yet.

"Yeah, I know. Like I told you though, no suffering, physically or emotionally. So, if she sleeps the whole way I'll feel better about it. I know it sounds kind of dumb, considering what I am about to do to her."

"I know," Marilyn said, cutting him off. "I was just teasing."

Marilyn rolled the unconscious girl on her belly and opened a small duffel bag. She took out a set of handcuffs and clicked them onto Jackie's delicate wrists. Marilyn bound the girl's ankles and knees together with duct tape, cutting the tape with scissors after several loops. She rolled her onto her back and packed her mouth with another rag, sealing it in place with several strips of tape.

She took some pictures of her, then covered her with a bed sheet that was folded in the corner. Then she sat back and relaxed with their catch, keeping a close eye on her for any movement. If necessary, she would knock her out again with the chloroform.

* * *

Bruce took the day off from the office. He was so excited, he didn't care if the company burned down. He checked the time. By now, they should have at least made contact with her and had her in the minivan.

Little thing had her whole life ahead of her. Oh well. So it goes.

He was in the basement making sure that everything was set for their young guest of honor today. The large table in the middle of the room was now equipped with metal cuffs attached to each of the eyebolts. About ten feet to the left of the table was a plastic portable tub with a fifteen-gallon capacity, a rolled up tarp, and a long rectangular folding table. On the table were two aluminum roasting pans and Chris's butcher kit.

About fifteen feet away were two folding lounge chairs with a small table in between them, a $2,000 bottle of Cabernet Sauvignon and two long stem glasses.

Something nice for such a special occasion.

Bruce's phone beeped. It was a photo message from his wife containing two pictures. The first was a close-up of Jackie Nixon's face. She was asleep with her mouth taped shut. The second photo was a full body shot. Her hands were cuffed behind her back, and her knees and ankles were bound together with duct tape. Like they had agreed, her Catholic school uniform was left on. She'd be stripped here in the basement. A second text message from Marilyn followed.

"Stay home. I'm bringing dinner tonight :)"

CHAPTER 12

IT WAS 7:40 A.M. AND SARAH hadn't slept a wink. She had been fighting a cold the last two days, but last night it got progressively worse. She tossed and turned all night and could hardly breathe. Her nightstand was covered with used, rolled-up tissues. She hadn't called out of work yet, but today she would have to. At least it was Friday and not the middle of the week. She called Kevin.

"Hello?"

"Hey Kevin. It's Sarah."

"Oh, hey Sarah. You don't sound too good."

Sarah cleared her throat and snickered. "Yeah, I have this really crappy cold and a sore throat. Probably a fever too. I'm really sorry but I don't think I can come in today."

"No problem at all. Take care of yourself and relax. I'll stay a couple of extra hours and one of the techs can run things tonight."

"Thanks so much. I'll make it up to you. I don't have any surgeries or anything today. I think just one appointment."

"No need to make it up. You've been here every day. Just forget about this place and relax. We'll hold down the fort."

"Okay. Thanks so much."

"Feel better."

"Thanks. See you Monday."

The next phone call was to her mother. She didn't work Fridays and Saturdays so she asked her through a series of sniffles if she could make a pot of her famous chicken noodle soup, guaranteed to knock any sickness out. Her mother was more than happy to make the soup, and would be at Sarah's around noon.

Sarah had a few hours to try and get some sleep. But first she spent a few minutes checking her Facebook feed, "liked" a few posts, then checked her e-mail and saw that she had a new message on OKCupid. She rolled her eyes and wondered why she bothered, since so far it had been a complete waste of time, but she clicked on the link to read it.

Sean85
32 / M / Straight / Single
New York, NY

Subject -Hey There

Sarah,

Just wanted to say a quick hello since I really enjoyed your profile. You made me laugh a few times and perhaps most importantly I am also a cheese aficionado. So we would definitely hit it off, haha.

Honestly, I never know what to say in these messages but you seem like the kind of person who would appreciate something more than "Hey let's hang out." So a little more about me . . .

1. I'm a lawyer, but not the kind that everyone hates who gets people out of jail. I deal in finances. So hopefully "lawyer" isn't a deal breaker.

2. I don't live with my mom.

3. I love Sci-Fi especially older stuff. I could watch an all day Twilight Zone marathon on that rainy day you mentioned.

4. I also love animals. I think you have a cool profession but I'm sure it gets difficult sometimes. My parents have a dog, but my apartment in the city doesn't allow them. Unacceptable, but I'm stuck here for the moment.

5. With the politics, we'd get along. I'm not too much into it either, but some of what's going on with this president just gets me outraged sometimes.

Anyway, there's more in my profile which I hope you'll check out. You seem really down to earth, and you have an absolutely gorgeous smile. Hope to hear back from you!

-Sean

PS: Happy belated birthday! Hope it was awesome. (saw you were an Aries)

Sarah clicked on his profile and saw that he was presentable and handsome. He seemed to be a big baseball fan, and he rooted for the New York Mets. She was okay with that. She wasn't really into sports but she did like the Mets. This was the first time she'd felt good after reading a message, so she could deal with his passion for baseball. She wrote back right away.

SarahMCC89
30 / F / Straight / Single
Long Island, NY

Subject - Re: Hey There

Sean,

Thank you for that message :) And thanks for noticing my birthday. How observant! It was a lot of fun, thanks. The next morning? Not so much. Speaking of being sick, at the moment, I am kinda sorta severely under the weather, but your message definitely made my morning! I'll totally write back with a little more hopefully tomorrow, or whenever I feel a little better. Also, I totally get what you said about being outraged. Since last November I seriously feel embarrassed sometimes to be an American. I try to not let it get to me, but sometimes it's really hard.

Anyway, I'll write back again soon. I promise :)

-Sarah

* * *

Jennifer showered after her quick morning workout. Today was a casual Friday in the office because there was a company outing at tonight's Yankee game. Jennifer didn't know much at all about baseball, but once a year her boss bought a suite at Yankee Stadium and had a party for some of his employees and even a few clients. She'd had a lot of fun last year and drank a little too much, but she was very excited about going tonight. She'd heard that the Yankees were a good team this year too.

After dressing she checked her e-mail to see if there was anything urgent that needed an immediate response. She skimmed through a few messages but there was nothing pressing and she would respond when she got to the office. She checked the time and decided to make a quick breakfast. Since she was leaving a little early tonight she figured that she might have to work through lunch, so she whipped up some scrambled eggs, toast and tea.

When she got to work, she made a cup of coffee, sat in her office and spent a half hour reading financial news and updates. On days like today with no client meetings scheduled, she would pick out files of one or two of her clients, review them, and continue to design and map out their financial futures. She'd play out different scenarios: what would happen if the money was moved here? Or there? If she had any new suggestions, she would call them directly and explain her thought process in a way that they could understand. She was good at that.

Her boss knocked on the door and popped in.

"You coming to the stadium tonight, Jen?"

"Yep! I'll be there. Looking forward to it."

"Good, are you bringing anyone?"

"Nope, just me."

He marked her off on a list and gave her one ticket.

"A couple of potential heavy hitters will be there tonight as guests. They're looking for new advisors. If it's alright with you I'd like you to meet them. I think you'd be a good fit for them."

"Oh sure, I'd love to. Thanks!"

Something to take my attention away from a boring baseball game.

"You got it, Jen. Clients rave about you so I'm going to start throwing some more stuff at you."

She thanked him again and before she got back to work, she looked up what was going on with the Yankees. They were playing the Baltimore Orioles tonight. She didn't want to seem completely clueless in case these heavy hitters she was going to meet tonight were big baseball fans. She couldn't care less about baseball, but she'd be prepared.

For the rest of the afternoon she analyzed portfolios. After speaking with a few of her clients, she shut down for the weekend and split a cab to the ballpark with two of her co-workers.

By the time she arrived at Yankee Stadium and went through the turnstile at Gate 4, an innocent young high school girl had been brutally slaughtered about two and a half hours away.

CHAPTER 13

BRUCE WAS WAITING OUTSIDE when the minivan pulled onto the property and into the open garage. His erection felt like it would burst through his jeans. He shut the garage door and shook hands with Chris. Bruce walked around to the passenger side where his wife already had the sliding door open. She pulled off the bed sheet and Bruce got his first up-close look at Jackie Nixon. She was bound and gagged just as she had been in the photos.

Marilyn explained that it had taken about two minutes to knock her out, and she had started to stir a bit after thirty minutes but she was instantly put back to sleep with another small dose of chloroform. Before they arrived, she had hit her with a third dose.

"I'd say we have about thirty or forty minutes before she wakes up," she said.

"Can you guys bring her in? I have to take a leak and get myself set up downstairs," Chris said.

"Yeah, we got her," Marilyn replied.

Chris reached into the vehicle and took Jackie's book bag and her shoes, which had fallen off during the struggle. He brought those items in with him and Marilyn turned back to Bruce.

"It was the biggest thrill of my life. Knocking her out. Jesus Christ. You ready to bring her in?"

Bruce chuckled and replied, "I've only been waiting my whole life. Yes, I think I'm ready."

He took hold of her ankles and dragged the unconscious soccer star to the edge of the opening so that he could lean in, scoop her up and cradle-carry her into the house. Marilyn followed him through the side garage door, down a hallway, past the kitchen and past one of the outlets to the back yard where a large grill sat. He looked down at the peacefully sleeping girl, still having a hard time believing that she would be served for dinner tonight after being cooked on that grill.

Meat is meat, he remembered Chris saying. Just as people hunted deer, they hunted.

It's the natural order of things. We are higher up on the chain than she is. It's as simple as that.

It made sense to him and Marilyn now. Chris vowed to do an outstanding job and promised that they would enjoy his niece when she was served. Marilyn knew that if they did, they would have to incorporate the butchering, cooking, and eating of their victim for the event.

After everyone has their way with her, of course. Jackie here will have it relatively easy.

Marilyn led the way down to the basement. He was very careful, taking the stairs slowly and one step at a time. She opened the heavy door at the base of the stairwell and Bruce carried Jackie in. Finally, the basement torture chamber would be christened with its first victim. He placed her face up on the large table in the center of the room, then rolled her onto her belly. Marilyn had the key ready, and she uncuffed the wrists. Bruce rolled her back over as Chris walked in carrying Jackie's book bag and shoes.

"We're trashing all of this, right?"

"Yes, we'll get rid of it all," Marilyn replied.

Chris placed the items in a black trash bag and joined Bruce and Marilyn. They cuffed the girl's wrists to the top corners of the table using the metal handcuffs that were attached to the eyebolts. The tape binding her ankles and knees was cut, and Bruce removed her knee-high socks, tossed them on the floor and he and Marilyn each cuffed one of her ankles to the bottom corners. All three took a moment to run their hands over her body.

"These legs are just perfect. Well-toned, very nice cuts from the thighs," Chris said as he gave her right thigh a light slap.

"How long will you need before we hang her up?" he asked Bruce.

"Not long at all. We just want to make sure the table is solid, and we want to make sure we can't hear her screaming from outside of this room. Five, ten minutes, then she's all yours," Bruce replied.

"Good. I want to end it quickly."

"Not a problem. I'll be ready with the hammer," Bruce said.

Marilyn tapped Bruce on the shoulder. He turned and saw her holding the bottle of wine.

"Celebratory toast?"

"Yes of course," Bruce responded. "Would you like a glass?" he asked Chris.

"No thanks, I'll take a beer though. Oh, and I'll need two plastic bags, to cover my shoes."

Marilyn retrieved a beer and the bags from the kitchen upstairs. Bruce poured two glasses of wine and handed one to his wife. Chris cracked open his Budweiser and they raised their drinks.

"Chris, this is to you. Thank you for reaching out and giving us this fantastic opportunity at the expense of your niece. I know a part of you has to find this difficult, but we can't say enough about how much we appreciate this," Bruce toasted.

"And I'm drinking to you two. You are the ones really making this happen and making my dream a reality. Cheers guys."

They all took a healthy sip of their drinks Marilyn looked down at the unconscious girl, then looked back up and continued:

"Jackie sounded like a really great girl. You were brave to do this and like Bruce said, and I can see it too, it has to be a little hard."

"Yeah, it is a little bit. That's why I want to end it quickly. Once she's dead I'll be fine. It'll just be a carcass to cut up and process. No different than a deer. Well, a little different. And yes, she was a really great girl with her whole life ahead of her. But this had to be done. Plain and—"

He was interrupted by the sound of metal clanking, followed by a piercing, high-pitched scream. It was music to Bruce and Marilyn's ears. They put their glasses down and approached Jackie. Her eyes were darting around the room, looking at each of the four restraints as she struggled fiercely. She could see herself in the mirror on the ceiling. Chris took another drink of his beer and watched.

"Well *hello,* darlin'," Marilyn said as she stroked her cheek and wiped away a tear. Jackie let out another round of horrified screams when Bruce groped her breasts. Chris stepped closer into her field of view. They briefly made eye contact, and then he looked away and took another drink as she yelled at him for help through the gag.

"Oh, your uncle is helping you plenty. Believe me, sweetie pie. You are *so* fortunate that he's here. This would be *much* harder for you if he wasn't."

When Bruce finished fondling her and while Marilyn continued to taunt her, he took a moment to check each of the four eyebolts to see how they were holding up with Jackie fighting to break free. All four were holding perfectly. Marilyn stepped away from the table and Bruce unlocked the mechanism that allowed the table to tilt forward to roughly a 60 degree angle. She looked at her uncle again and begged him for help. She could now see herself in the wall mirror directly across from her. Bruce noted that considering the way she was stretched out and as the result of simple gravity, her wrists must have been in excruciating pain.

He went into the closet and fetched a pair of trauma sheers. He held them up in front of Jackie's face.

"What do you say we get these silly clothes off you?"

She screamed "no" and cried hysterically as he sliced away her skirt, tossing the remnants on the floor. Without much delay, he cut her shirt from the bottom, right up to the middle and tore it off, revealing a white bra. Jackie continued to fight, but she was completely helpless as he snipped away at her bra and lavender panties, exposing her shaved pubic area.

Moments after being stripped of her clothes, from sheer terror and the resulting loss of control, Jackie let loose a stream of urine. Bruce and Marilyn laughed at her. Sweat and tears streamed down her face. Bruce slid the scissors into his back pocket and savagely fondled her, squeezing her firm, but supple breasts. Marilyn left the basement and shut the door. Bruce stuck two fingers up her vagina and briefly finger-fucked her, inducing another round of earsplitting screams.

Marilyn returned.

"Did you hear anything?" Bruce asked.

"Not a fucking thing," Marilyn responded with a smile.

Bruce nodded to Chris. Plastic bags covered his shoes and goggles rested on top of his head. He was wearing a black rubber apron and latex gloves.

"You ready for her?"

"Yep, I'm all set. Let's get her up," Chris said.

Marilyn took a few photos of Jackie with the high-definition camera, taunting her and telling her to smile before each shot. When she finished, Bruce tilted the table back again so that she faced the ceiling. He lowered the hoist from the ceiling, guiding the spreader bar towards Jackie's feet. He nodded to Marilyn, who uncuffed Jackie's left ankle and wrestled it into the leather cuff attached to the left end of the spreader bar. They repeated the process with her right ankle and tightened both cuffs.

Marilyn uncuffed the girl's wrists and Bruce pulled on the rope to slowly hoist her up while she frantically screamed and flailed her arms. She begged them not to hurt her as the pulley locked in place. Marilyn and Bruce took control of her arms and cuffed her hands behind her back. Bruce unlocked the wheels on the table and rolled it aside. He slid the folding table carrying Chris's butcher kit and the aluminum pans next to her. He lightly slapped her ass twice and then stepped back to take in the sight.

Hanging upside down by her feet, her ponytail pointed to the floor. Her body jerked and twitched as she tried frenetically to fight free. She tilted her head forward and was looking up at her feet, desperately attempting to find a way out. The experience to this point for Bruce and Marilyn was already spectacular, yet a small part of them felt guilt and remorse, and they read this in each other's eyes. They were not animals, had not fully lost touch with their humanity. But a bigger part of them was thrilled. They were about to murder an innocent 18-year-old girl, and her terror was at a level beyond description. They were of one mind in this.

This is why we were put on this earth. This is why we crossed paths. For this moment. This is supposed to happen.

Marilyn sat in one of the folding chairs enjoying a clear view of Jackie's body. Bruce topped off their wine and then retrieved a hammer out of the closet. Chris was kneeling next to his niece and whispering to her. Bruce gave him a moment.

"I am sorry, honey. I really am. But things are happening that are bigger than you and me. I'm sorry I'm not the person you thought I was. I promise your family won't know how bad it was and how scared you were, and I'm going to make it as painless as possible."

He kissed her on the cheek, causing her to cry uncontrollably. He licked his lips and tasted a salty combination of sweat and tears on his tongue.

"Take a minute if you want to say a prayer, sweetheart. It'll be over very soon."

He put the goggles on and opened the butcher's kit, which Jackie could see out of the corner of her eye. She immediately looked away. A carving knife and fork, a boning knife, a paring knife, a meat cleaver, shears, and a slicer were neatly arranged in the case.

He nodded at Bruce who stood behind her. She never saw it coming. He struck the back of her head with the hammer, knocking her out instantly. She bled from the point of impact, but was still alive. Bruce and Chris laid out the tarp on the floor beneath her and then Chris slid the tub underneath her head.

Bruce took his seat alongside Marilyn. Chris took the boning knife in one hand. With the other, he pulled up her ponytail, fully exposing her neck. He diagramed the cut mentally, then stuck the knife to the jugular vein and made a deep cut. He continued to cut across the length of her neck. Blood splashed his apron, followed by a steady flow into the tub. Jackie's body twitched and convulsed as she slowly bled out. Chris stepped away and finished his beer, watching alongside Bruce and Marilyn as Jackie's life ended.

Now, it was all business.

"Just a disclaimer," he started, "obviously this is going to be a bit messy. I also wanted to point out that normally the carcass would be gutted and split, and then hung in a cooler for about two days. That ages the meat and tenderizes it. I'll spare you the science lesson. But she'll be fine to cook today. I just want to leave the meat seasoning for a few hours and we'll get her on the grill in time for dinner. It'll really just be the legs, the ass, and her biceps. The organs aren't anything special. Humans weren't meant to be raised for meat, but there will be enough to fill us up."

Bruce and Marilyn watched intently as Chris expertly performed his craft. Their basement was now an abattoir. After the carcass was bled out, he cut around the rest of her neck and decapitated her. He placed her head in one of the pans. The mouth was still gagged, and her face appeared to be frozen in that final moment of terror. He then split the chest cavity and belly open and cut around inside, allowing the intestines to spill out into the tub.

"All in all, it's going to take an hour and a half, two hours to get her skinned, quartered, and butchered."

He uncuffed the wrists from behind the back, allowing the arms to dangle. He hosed the carcass down, took the paring knife and began to skin the body from top to bottom, starting with the left ankle.

* * *

They continued eating the steaks that had been carved from Jackie's thighs, and there was more meat ready to go on the grill. Keeping in mind the old cliché "presentation is everything," Chris used Jackie's head as the centerpiece of the dinner table, decorated with a wreath around it. The tape and gag had been removed, but the lifeless eyes were still open, looking straight ahead at the people dining on her body. Bruce and Marilyn raved about the taste and quality of the meat. Chris did not appear to be the least bit shaken by the brutal murder of his niece. He was not at all bothered by this married couple cutting their "Jackie steaks" into smaller pieces before savagely devouring them.

"I've got to hand it to you, chef. You've made us believers!" Bruce said as he wiped his mouth.

"Thanks very much. I'm glad you enjoyed it. Anyone want seconds?"

"Absolutely, but let's talk a little business first," Bruce said. "First of all, if you still want to come to the event, we'd love to have you. Just keep in mind that it's going to be different from today, because the girl will be tortured before she's handed over to you. You wouldn't take part in any of that. Your job would just be to butcher and cook her after everyone has their way with her. Is that fair?"

"That's fine with me. Actually, would it be possible to kidnap two women? I don't know what kind of a crew you have, but just throwing it out there. You could have one of them in the basement being tortured, and give me the other one to prepare in the meantime. The guests could have dinner right after the torture. If suffering is your priority, I have an idea."

They were intrigued. "What do you have in mind?" Marilyn asked.

Chris looked out towards the vast back yard.

"You'd have to do a little digging outside, and we'd need a few things. A fifteen-foot metal pole, preferably steel or titanium. Let's do a little walk-through in the back yard when we're done eating. I have something like a luau in mind."

CHAPTER 14

MONDAY MAY 1, 2017

After a long weekend cleaning up, Bruce sat in his office exhausted. The remains of Jackie Nixon and her organs, along with her clothing and her belongings, had been disposed of in a burn barrel and set on fire in the back yard on Saturday morning. The ashy remnants were driven to a wooded area ten miles away and discarded. The blood in the plastic tub was poured down the drains in the basement floor. The tarp was hosed down and hung up to dry, and the slaughter area was bleached and hosed.

The first article about her disappearance appeared online late Saturday morning. Bruce and Marilyn hardly breathed as they read, but relaxed when they learned no suspects had been identified. They were sure that they had covered their tracks, and it was a relief to see that in writing.

Or not in writing.

After an early staff meeting, Bruce found the latest article on a Long Island newspaper website.

AUTHORITIES SUSPECT FOUL PLAY IN DISAPPEARANCE OF LONG ISLAND STUDENT: NO LEADS

Nassau County officials are expanding the search for a Long Island high school student who has not been seen since Friday morning, and have enlisted the assistance of the New York State Police.

Jackie Nixon, 18, was reported missing after she was last seen by her father when she left for school Friday morning. Officials suspect foul play, but at this point no persons of interest have been identified and no significant leads have been provided.

"Our chief concern is the safe return of Miss Nixon," lead detective Vincent Flynn said, "but we are proceeding under the theory that she was abducted. We are currently devoting many resources including harbor, aviation, and canine into this search. We are

> *working around the clock."*
>
> *When asked why they suspected foul play, Detective Flynn cited interviews with Nixon's family and friends who said that it is highly unusual for her not to be in touch with anyone.*
>
> *"We are not talking about someone who has any history of mental illness. For her to just not show up at school and not tell anyone, for her phone to be off and untraceable, for her to not be in contact with anyone to this point, we believe that this was an abduction."*
>
> *Nixon's distraught parents have declined comment.*
>
> *"She is an absolute jewel and a blessing to everyone who knows her. She couldn't possibly hurt anyone. Whoever has her, please, please bring her back," a family friend who wished to remain anonymous said.*
>
> *Nixon, a varsity athlete and member of the National Honor Society, had committed to playing soccer at the University of Pittsburgh this fall. Anyone with any information on her whereabouts is urged to call 911 or the Nassau County Missing Persons Squad.*

Bruce exhaled as he finished reading. No suspects, no leads, and Marilyn had said there were absolutely no cameras in the area.

We're in the clear.

* * *

Sarah arrived to work an hour early on Monday. She figured she'd offer Kevin the chance to go home early since he'd covered for her a couple of hours on Friday night. She knocked on the door to his office.

"Hey Sarah! How are you feeling?"

"Still not a hundred percent, but much better, thanks. No headaches on Friday?"

"Nope. I stayed an hour and it was nice and slow. Veronica took over for the night and I was on standby for emergencies."

"Okay, great. If you want I can take over now, since you covered for me."

"No, it's okay. I've got to finish up some paperwork and it wasn't a problem. Go get some lunch or some coffee if you want."

Sarah saw the newspaper on his desk. A picture of the missing Long Island girl was on the front page.

"Terrible news about that girl. My God," Sarah said.

Kevin frowned. "I know. Heartbreaking. I have two young kids and I can't imagine what those parents are going through right now."

"I thought the same thing. Jesus. She's so beautiful too. She lives in the next town from me."

"I have my fingers crossed and I'm praying for her, but these things usually don't end well."

"I know. I'm praying for her too. Anyway, I'll be in the lounge if you need me."

"Okay, Sarah, thanks."

Sarah made herself a cup of coffee, sat at a table and as promised, sent Sean from OKCupid the follow up message.

* * *

Jennifer went online to check the stock markets before her three o'clock meeting with a client. Even the business websites had articles about the missing Long Island girl. She shook her head as she read one of the stories.

God, what is wrong with people?

Her heart ached as she thought of the girl's loved ones. She hoped that she was still alive, and that she would fight and by some miracle would eventually find herself home. She felt angry thinking about the person or persons responsible for the girl's disappearance, and hoped that they would be brought to justice.

They're right. There's no way she's a runaway. She was kidnapped.

Jennifer took a break from work and searched for more articles. She was upset that there were no suspects, let alone any leads whatsoever. Her office phone rang. It was a number she didn't recognize so she let it go to voicemail. All the Internet searches led her to a Facebook page that had just gone live an hour earlier.

FIND JACKIE NIXON

We are the family and closest friends of our dear Jackie. Thank you for the outpouring of love, support, and prayers for Jackie's safe return. Please share this page and stay tuned for updates.

For everyone who wants to help, there are a couple of ways you can do so. We have generated fliers with photos of Jackie along with information about her. The flier can be found in the photo album. If you can print some out and post them around your neighborhood it would be greatly appreciated.

The other way you can help is to donate to the GoFundMe page which is linked at the top. All money donated will go towards a reward for information leading to Jackie's safe return. Somebody out there knows something, and we hope this is a way they can come forward.

We'd like to thank all law enforcement involved in this case. We know we are getting their best effort.

Please keep Jackie and her parents in your prayers.

Jennifer took her credit card out and donated $500, with the message "You are all in my prayers." Then she listened to the voicemail. It was a potential new client. She ignored it for now, and prepped for her three o'clock meeting with a heavy heart.

CHAPTER 15

SATURDAY MAY 6, 2017

Sean picked an Italian restaurant in Manhattan's trendy Greenwich Village for their first date. He had offered to pick Sarah up from her home, but she didn't think that was appropriate yet so she politely declined. They seemed to have decent chemistry through Internet messaging and for the last two days, text messages, but her first face-to-face meeting someone from a dating website had her a bit nervous. Not that she was worried for her safety, she was just anxious that is could be very awkward.

The restaurant wasn't upscale, and they agreed to keep things casual. Sarah was pleased with that. It allowed her to wear something comfortable, which would make her feel more confident. For the first time in a while, she spent extra time with her hair and held it in place with hairspray.

If this turns into something, he'll know to appreciate when I do this.

She wore a pine green blouse, dark blue skinny jeans and flats. She was looking forward to what would hopefully be a fun and pleasant first date with good food, good wine, and good company after the earlier, somber events of the day.

She was still one stop away on the subway and she was three minutes late. She hadn't accounted enough for the weekend schedule. When the train pulled into her station, she got out and scurried up the stairs. Once she was at street level a little after seven o'clock her phone pinged with a text message from Sean.

"Got here a little early. No rush, take your time."

"Just got off the train. Be there in 5 min."

It was a cool, comfortable Saturday evening, which helped to calm her nerves. She hoped that this would work. She enjoyed being single and hanging out with her friends, but now that she was thirty years old, she wanted companionship and a real relationship. It was all that was missing in her life.

When she arrived on the block, she saw him standing outside. He greeted her with a smile and a warm hug as she approached.

"Hey, so nice to meet you! You look beautiful," he said.

"Thanks, you too! Well, handsome I mean. God I'm sorry I'm late. Trains kind of sucked."

"No problem. I just got here a few minutes ago. So, we have a table reserved. Shall we?"

"Yes," Sarah said with a radiant smile.

If first impressions meant anything, Sean was off to a great start. He was a couple of inches taller than her and she liked that. He had a great smile, he was handsome, and he dressed nicely with a clean, pressed button-down shirt and jeans. And best of all, she still could feel the tingle of excitement his hug had given her. She'd felt safe and snug in his arms and wanted to be there again.

Inside of the restaurant, he pulled her chair out before he took his seat.

The ambience was warm, and instrumental jazz played at a low volume over the speakers. The waitress introduced herself, and Sean ordered a bottle of Pinot Noir to start off with.

"So, lucky me. Sarah's first OKCupid date," Sean said.

"Yeah," Sarah said, "my first. And to be honest I never thought I'd meet anyone on that site. It seems to be more about casual hookups. But here we are!"

"Yep, here we are. Glad I found you before you ditched the site."

"Me too, *so far,*" she said teasingly. "How many people have you met?"

"A few. I think three actually, but nothing ever worked out. It's different meeting someone in person and sometimes the chemistry just isn't there. I haven't had a second date from that site."

"Well I never thought I'd resort to it, but so far I'm impressed."

"I'm glad you made the trip downtown. What else did you do with your day off?"

She thought about whether she should tell him the truth or just skirt it. She decided that there was no reason to lie.

"They had that vigil for that missing girl."

"Oh yes, of course. You went to that today?"

"Yeah, she lived in the next town over from me. I wasn't doing anything today so I just felt like I should go. It's such a tragic story."

"I know. It is really sad."

"It's such a scary thing. A beautiful and popular girl like that can go missing and they have, like, *nothing* and it's been over a week."

"For sure. This day and age for that to happen, it is very disturbing."

"The vigil was really emotional and so many people came out. I wish I could do more," Sarah said.

Sean took the lead and changed the subject. For the next hour and a half they talked about their jobs, their best friends, where they had traveled, their pet peeves, their favorite movies. The conversation flowed naturally with a balance of talking and listening from each of them. There was obvious chemistry. After dinner, they each ordered different desserts and shared them with one another.

Sarah had her mind made up that she wanted to see him again, but she didn't want to rush things.

"Any interest in hitting a bar?" Sean said after he handed his credit card to the waitress.

"I really can't. I have to get an early start tomorrow. I'm sorry! We should absolutely get together again though."

"I'd love to. Well at least let me drive you to Penn Station? It's on the way for me anyway."

"Okay, sure. That would be great."

The sun was down now and they walked to the parking garage around the block and the valet retrieved Sean's car, a black 2017 Mercedes.

"Nice ride," Sarah said.

He smiled and opened the passenger door for her. They continued to talk and laugh during the short ten-minute drive to Penn Station.

He's perfect.

"So, when can I see you again?" he asked.

"During the week is tough because of my hours, but I can meet you in the city for lunch. Other than that, weekends are usually good."

"Let's shoot for something next weekend then," Sean said as he pulled over outside of Penn.

"Definitely."

"And next time I'll pick you up, okay?"

"Sure. Sounds good."

Her plan was to take it slow, but her emotions got the best of her. She leaned over, made it obvious, and he reciprocated. It was a long, passionate kiss and they both knew that it would be the first of many.

"Good night," Sarah said as she opened the door.

"Good night, sweetheart. Text me when you get home?"

"I will."

The station was crowded but she felt alone, elated over her first date with Sean. From his good looks, to his clothes and his car, and even the way he carried himself, she liked everything about him.

And he likes me!

* * *

In the Hudson Valley, the meeting to decide on the victim was underway. Bruce, Marilyn, and the kidnap crew sat in the living room. Bruce had his laptop hooked up to the television.

"Before we start, we wanted to show you guys something."

He pulled up a video from a recent newscast and clicked "play." A female anchor spoke solemnly:

"Hundreds showed up at a prayer vigil for Jackie Nixon, the missing Long Island teen who has not been seen in eight days. Fliers were handed out by volunteers as the parents of the missing teen made their first public statement."

Pictures of Jackie, heartbreaking to most because she appeared so jubilant and full of life, were shown on the screen, and then the video cut to her visibly shaken father. The mother stood to his left wiping tears from her eyes.

"We just want our girl home. Whoever has her, please, we beg you to let her go. I don't know what you want from her, or from us, but please just let Jackie go."

The video ended with the news anchor updating the latest in the investigation which, in actuality, wasn't much of an update. Bruce closed the video.

"You guys ready for this? Drum roll please."

He clicked on a photo album, and pictures of Jackie naked, gagged, and restrained to the table in the basement filled the screen.

"Holy *fucking shit,*" Darryl said. His partners stared at the photos, rapt with attention.

"You guys did this?" Hank asked.

"Yes, but we had some help. The girl's uncle was actually the main player. We wanted to give the place a little dry run and he offered us the opportunity, so we took it," Bruce said.

"She's gone, right?" Darryl asked.

"Oh yeah, she was dead a few hours after we got her," Bruce replied.

"Her uncle is a chef and a butcher," Marilyn said. "We strung her up in the basement and he slaughtered her and chopped up her body like a pig."

"And then we grilled some steaks and had dinner."

Darryl and his team visibly squirmed. Bruce and Marilyn spoke as if what had happened was nothing more than a run-of-the-mill family cookout.

"Jesus fucking Christ," Darryl said. "We all heard about her on the news but I had no idea."

"Yeah, it was a sudden thing and we kept it under wraps," Bruce said.

"The body, the rest of it. What did you do with it?" Willie asked.

"We burned it along with all her stuff and dumped the ashes about ten miles away. We're good. You've seen the news. They have nothing," Marilyn said.

"So, you guys butchered and cooked her. I have to ask, how did it taste?" Darryl asked.

"It was outstanding," Bruce said. "Had a little bit of a pork flavor, but definitely distinct and different."

"I was squeamish at first, but like he said, it was delicious," Marilyn said. "So anyway, we're telling you this because we want to talk about the possibility of you guys kidnapping two girls instead of one."

Bruce added, "We'd be able to significantly increase the minimum bid for the auction which of course means more money in all of our pockets. Our idea is that Chris, the butcher slash chef, would prepare and cook one girl for dinner while the other is being tortured."

Darryl and his men talked amongst themselves, and decided that they would likely be able to kidnap two women, but there were a lot of factors at play. Just like before, they would split up in teams of two and continuously watch the women who were selected.

"The proximity of the abductions. You'd want them at about the same time, right?" Darryl asked.

"Ideally, yes. Not necessarily the same day, but we want to notify the winners once both women are in our custody so they can make their travel plans. We'd want to have the event a day or two after we have both of them here," Bruce explained.

"Here's what we'll do. First, let's decide on the two. Me and my guys will watch each one. Give us about a month, and ideally we'd find the perfect time to split up and grab both the same day. Or worst-case scenario, we grab one, and then the other the next day," Darryl said.

"Good. Everyone knows the risks involved here, and they know that dates are very flexible and can be changed at the last second, so none of that will be an issue," Bruce said.

"And no one comes until we are paid in full," Marilyn added.

The meeting shifted to the dining room where the files on the ten women were laid out on the table. Bruce and Marilyn suggested that Darryl and his team go through them and tell them which ones involved the lowest risk.

"This one here, the mom in Queens. I think she'd be the easiest. She's a stay-at-home mother and we'd likely grab her right out of the house while the husband is at work, but we'd have to take the kid too. He's old enough to understand what would be happening. If you're comfortable with that, she could be one," Darryl said.

"Here's another one. The teacher in Staten Island. Could be easy to grab on her jogging route," Hank said.

"The ones who live alone are always less risky," Tom explained. "This one here, you guys have a lot of info on her." He held up the file on Sarah McConnell.

"What are your thoughts on kidnapping her? She has this thing about her. I can't put my finger on it, but I really like her and she might have the perfect body for Chris," Marilyn said.

"She's likely doable. She does live alone," Darryl said.

"The fact that she works nights helps a lot too. She takes the train to Long Island and when she gets off, she walks to her car and there is *no one* around. I think she's definitely doable," Hank added.

"Let's make her one of the choices then. I do like her too," Bruce said.

"Okay, we got her. Now, for number two," Darryl said.

"Let's stay away from the Queens mother if we can. She looks amazing, but I don't want to get the kid involved," Marilyn said.

"Not a problem. As far as the ones who live alone, it's the teacher in Staten Island and this one here. She also lives in Queens and she works at a big Midtown firm. She's certainly a possibility as long as we can grab her out of the home."

"Her name is Jennifer. She's the one I chatted with on her birthday," Willie added.

"She is a lot prettier than the teacher. Nice and tall too. I think people would bid good money to have her," Marilyn said. She and the men turned to Bruce.

"If you guys can do it, I'm onboard with her," Bruce said.

As quickly as that, the two targets were selected.

"Alright then boys," Darryl said.

"Time to hunt."

CHAPTER 16

SATURDAY MAY 13, 2017

Gizmo was lounging on one of her shoes.

"Mommy's going out with her boyfriend tonight!"

Well, not 'boyfriend' yet.

She picked Gizmo up and put him on the bed. She was giddy. They had texted back and forth every day this week and had made plans for tonight. Ever the attentive gentleman, he knew that she loved live music, so he had purchased two tickets for dinner and a show at a nearby Long Island jazz club. Her phone pinged with a text from Allison.

"Boy toy spending the night?"

"NO!"

"Boooooo. When it happens I want details."

"At least you don't have to babysit me on weekends anymore :)"

"I love babysitting ur sexy self. Where r u going tonight?"

"Jazz club. He's picking me up."

"And he's going to drop u off and want to spend the night."

"Not tonight. I like him but I don't want to rush."

"NEXT TIME it better happen. And I want to be the maid of honor at the wedding."

"Shut up! Lol. I gotta get ready. Tell ur mom I said happy mothers day."

"He is cute. Have fun babe. You say the same to urs."

She listened to a 90s music playlist—first up on the shuffle was "Iris" by the Goo Goo Dolls—while she got dressed and did her hair. She sat on her bed and checked her Facebook timeline while she waited, and then Sean texted her that he was outside.

"Mommy will be back. Be a good kitty while I'm gone."

* * *

Darryl had the current twelve-hour shift by himself and sat outside. With two targets on the radar, the four men did a lot of the watching individually. It was the best way to make sure the women were being watched around the clock.

He saw a man in a black Mercedes pull up in front of the woman's house, and two minutes later she came out. He took the camera, zoomed in and snapped a few pictures of her.

Our lady has a boyfriend?

He opened the new notebook dedicated to Sarah McConnell and made an entry with the date and time she left her house. He also jotted down the Mercedes vehicle information, and then followed them from a safe distance. They arrived at a jazz club, and a valet took the car to park it.

A boyfriend could complicate things a bit.

* * *

Sean and Sarah sat on the same side of a table, facing the stage where a band was passionately playing a Duke Ellington tribute. They were close enough to see the sweat pouring down the saxophonist's face. Sarah raised her glass of wine, drank the little bit that was left. Sean wrapped his arms around her and kissed her neck as she leaned against him.

Sarah closed her eyes, completely lost in the moment. She listened to the band play while enjoying the sensation of being in the arms of a good, smart, strong man. She had longed for this, and wished this feeling at this moment would last forever. She felt chills all over as he gently caressed her and kissed the top of her head.

She opened her eyes when the audience started clapping after the final number. She smiled at Sean before sitting up and joining the round of applause. That was just to fit in. She hadn't really heard much of what was being played. She was in her own state of nirvana in Sean's arms.

The club host wished them a good night, and they walked arm-in-arm to the parking area. Sean handed the valet the ticket for his car.

"I had so much fun. Thank you so much," Sarah said as she leaned in for a long, passionate kiss.

"Of course, sweetheart. It's your company that makes it fun for me," Sean replied.

On the drive home, Sean held the wheel with one hand and massaged her neck with the other.

"So, when can I see you again?" he asked.

"As soon as possible?"

"I'm going to the Mets game next Saturday night with my brother and

Sunday is my dad's birthday. Maybe we can squeeze something in."

"Maybe we can meet for lunch next week? I'd love to go to a Mets game sometime too. I've gone to a few games and they're much more fun in person."

"Really? Definitely, we'll hit one up then. I'm a little busy during the week so I'm not sure if lunch will work. We'll figure something out for sure though."

"Yeah, we'll figure something out," Sarah said as Sean pulled up to her house.

He put the car in park and they fervidly kissed again. Sarah moaned as he squeezed one of her breasts.

"I don't want to be pushy, but . . ." Sean said, putting the ball in her court.

"I can't tonight. I really like you but I have to get an early start tomorrow."

"*Please,*" he jokingly begged.

Sarah laughed.

"I really can't. It's the whole Mother's Day thing, and I just want to take things a little slow. I love talking to you and spending time with you. I just don't do things like this all that often, and I want to do it at my own pace. I'm sorry."

"It's okay, I understand. I like you too, Sarah. You're so down to earth about everything. I love your company."

"Text me later?"

"I will. Good night, sweetheart."

"Goodnight."

They kissed one more time before he left. She walked into her house, tossed her keys on the dining room table and went right to the bedroom, plopped into bed and stared at the ceiling. Part of her was thrilled. She thought that she might be falling in love, but another part of her felt embarrassed that she didn't invite him in. Every part of her wanted to forget about taking things slowly, but she was worried about her performance. She hadn't had sex since college and she was afraid he would think she was so bad in bed that he wouldn't want to see her anymore.

Get a grip. Don't be ridiculous.

She slid her shoes off and curled under the covers with her clothes still on. She thought about the feeling of being wrapped in his arms, and slowly drifted to sleep.

* * *

"What a pussy," Darryl said as Sarah's date pulled away.

He decided not to follow him. After thinking it over, even if these two did start to see each other more frequently, it likely wouldn't be an issue. They had an idea in place already.

He spent a minute updating the notebook and then checked the time. He had three hours before Hank took over at two in the morning. The lights in the house went out, and it seemed that she was in for the night. He turned on the sports talk radio station but couldn't concentrate on it because his mind was venturing ahead to the time and place of her kidnapping. He tried to picture how it would go down, particularly the part after the delivery to Bruce and Marilyn—the good part where he gets to rape the fuck out of that bitch.

He grew hard imagining her naked and tied up. He had his own idea of how she should be restrained for him. He'd prefer her gagged. He didn't know what the others wanted. Maybe they'd want to hear her beg, maybe not. He'd want to fuck her at least twice. He'd be happy with that, and he imagined that the other three would be too. Then there was that other, much hotter girl. He hoped for two shots with her too.

Then he thought about what Bruce and Marilyn had planned for the girls.

Man, that is going to be brutal.

* * *

Jennifer worked all day Saturday at home, reviewing the files of the power players she'd been introduced to at Yankee Stadium two weeks earlier. There was a big meeting Monday morning and she wanted to be well-prepared, but she needed everything ready tonight because of Mother's Day tomorrow.

A lot of money was at stake and she was stressed out. She needed a distraction to clear her mind, so she arranged the paperwork into a neat pile and got dressed for a run. She tied her hair into a ponytail, laced up her running shoes and went for a late night jog. She'd work up a nice sweat, take a shower, and then plug away for a couple more hours.

* * *

"Where you goin' honey? You never run this late," Tom said out loud to himself.

He took a few photos of her but decided not to follow her. There was no need, since this wasn't part of her usual routine. He wrote in her notebook:

11:47 pm—leaves for jog

12:35 am—returns home from jog

One o'clock in the morning and the lights were still on. Maybe she was working late. The biggest problem with abducting her was the unpredictability of her hours. Some days she left the office at six, other nights she worked until eight or nine. One thing that was constant was that every Saturday and Sunday morning she would go out for a long run. Tom and the guys had her general route mapped out, so that was a possibility.

He thought about the plan, then looked at the photos he had just snapped of her. He saw dollar signs over this girl's head. She was going to be a huge payday.

Not "if." "When." We'll fucking get her.

CHAPTER 17

SUNDAY JUNE 11, 2017

Bruce was ready for Chris's help, so he took a few days off from work, loaded up the minivan with the equipment, and made the drive to the Hudson Valley. He arrived just after one in the afternoon.

"Just pull right into the back yard!" Bruce yelled.

Chris parked the car about twenty feet from an area that was dug out and marked off. Bruce reached into a cooler on the patio and pulled out a can of Bud Light.

"Welcome back my friend," Bruce said as he handed him the beer and greeted him with a hug.

"Great to be back! I see what you did over there. Looks great."

"Yeah, I dug it out about a foot deep. It's twelve feet long, four feet wide."

"It looks perfect. I think it'll do the job."

Marilyn came outside and greeted Chris with a hug and a kiss on the cheek.

"Welcome back. I'm sorry I can't hang today. We're having our crew over tonight for a meeting and I'm getting everything set. What is your availability for the weekend of July fifteenth?" she asked.

"Should be good to go. I'll clear that weekend. Is that when it's going down?"

"That's the date we're shooting for. That'll give everyone enough notice too. By the way, how are you doing? No problems, right?" she asked.

"Nope, never questioned by anyone. Seems like it finally died down a bit. My sister and her husband are obviously devastated but I think they've resigned themselves to the fact that she's gone and she ain't coming home."

"Very good. We haven't had any problems either. Feels good to know that we're in the clear, doesn't it?"

"Absolutely."

"Well, I'll let you boys get to it. Got a lot to do."

Marilyn went back into the house and Chris opened the sliding door of his minivan. The back was loaded with cinder blocks and other materials, and a long metal pole, which Chris pulled out first.

"Fifteen-feet long, titanium," Chris said as he placed it on the grass.

"Nice," Bruce said.

"And five crossbars," Chris said as he retrieved the other poles, much shorter in length. He placed them on the grass next to the long pole.

"How tall is the girl?" Chris asked.

"She's close to six feet, probably a shade under."

"Good. The pit is plenty long enough. Want to give me a hand with these?"

They placed flagstones on the outer edge of the pit. The cinder blocks were arranged around the perimeter of the stones, and mortar mix held them together.

"This keeps the heat in and the fire controlled," Chris explained.

On three sides of the pit, the blocks were stacked three high. On one of the long sides, they left an open area in the middle about six feet long with only one row of blocks. Once the simple but laborious construction was complete, Chris pushed on the cinder block walls until he was satisfied that they would not fall over or cave in. On each end of the pit, Chris used a circular saw with a masonry blade to cut out a groove six inches down into the blocks. He and Bruce then took each end of the fifteen-foot pole and place it into the grooves. It was a perfect fit.

"Now, just a crank to attach to one of the ends, and we're all set," Chris said.

"That wasn't so bad, actually," Bruce replied as he opened a new beer.

"Do you guys get any air traffic over here?" Chris asked.

"Absolutely nothing. Totally dead up here."

"A canopy might be a good idea, just in case. We wouldn't want anyone seeing what's going on from above. Also in case it rains."

"That's a good thought," Bruce acknowledged.

The completed barbecue pit was four and a half feet high, including the one foot that was dug out of the ground.

"Oh my God, it's beautiful!" Marilyn said when she came out.

"Thanks. It'll do the job just fine. I'll use either coal or wood for the fire. I haven't decided yet," Chris said.

"It'll work though, right? We're not just burning her quickly at the stake," Marilyn said.

"Yes, it will work. The most important thing will be keeping the heat extremely low. I'll take care of that. It will take a long time to cook her through, but it'll be quite a spectacle."

* * *

Sarah's phone pinged as she put the chicken parmesan in the oven. It was a text message from Sean.

"About ten minutes out"

"Come right in, the door is open :)"

Although they had spoken a lot over the past few weeks, they hadn't seen each other since the jazz club. Sean had been extremely busy at work, and then he'd taken a spur of the moment week long vacation with his brother. Once they were able to connect, Sarah suggested he come over for dinner and they could watch a movie on Netflix.

She was ready tonight.

She took a cheese platter out of the refrigerator, put it on the kitchen counter and checked on the chicken. Then she lit the two candles on the dinner table.

Soon after, the door opened and Sean walked in holding a bottle of red wine.

"Why thank you, how thoughtful," Sarah said before they hugged and kissed.

"You look lovely. Smells good!"

"It'll be ready in a couple of minutes. Help yourself to some of this incredible assortment of cheese. I hope you're hungry because dinner probably sucks. I warned you, I'm not a great cook," Sarah said.

Sean laughed. "I love chicken parmesan, though. I'm sure it'll be great. Where are your wine glasses?"

"Up in that cabinet. I'll open the bottle."

Sarah poured two glasses, handing one to the man she hoped would be hers. She hadn't seen him in almost a month, and she'd missed him terribly.

They made small talk and caught up on their professional and personal lives while they ate dinner. The pasta was soggy and the chicken was overcooked, and they both knew it was bad but he complimented her anyway. Just once. She appreciated his unspoken honesty.

He's so nice.

"You want to top off the wine? I'll put the dishes where, the washer?" Sean asked when they finished dinner.

"Oh, I got it, don't worry."

"No, no, I'll take care of the dishes."

"Thank you. Yes, the dishwasher."

Sarah filled the glasses and when he was done putting the dishes away, she took him by the hand and led him to the couch. They decided to put a comedy on, but Sarah didn't really care what they watched and she figured he didn't either. They took their shoes off and Sarah leaned against him on the couch. He put an arm around her.

Gizmo jumped onto the couch, head-butted Sarah's thigh and tried to nestle his way onto her lap. They both laughed. Sean patted him for a minute.

"This is Gizmo and he needs to get going," Sarah set Gizmo on the floor, and he nonchalantly strolled away.

They watched about twenty minutes of the movie before Sean made his move. He leaned over and kissed her, running his hands up her body and caressing her breasts. Sarah let out a long, fervent moan. She wasn't going to say "no" tonight. The television stayed on with the movie playing and after a few minutes of light foreplay on the couch, Sarah led him into the bedroom.

* * *

Darryl and his men were up in the Hudson Valley for their meeting with Bruce and Marilyn. Solid plans were in place. Marilyn asked them if the weekend of July fifteenth would work.

"We all good for that weekend guys?" Darryl asked.

The three men agreed. Darryl then laid out the plan.

"As far as Sarah goes, she's been seeing someone here and there. Not sure of their relationship status. Whatever the case, it won't affect our plan. It would be late at night, around two in the morning near the station. It'll be a military-type snatch and grab right off the street. Three of us would have to be there. We can do it that Friday night slash Saturday morning."

Bruce and Marilyn nodded their approval, and Darryl continued.

"The only problem is the other girl. The best time to get her would be at her house very early Saturday morning, around five. She lives on a very quiet block in Queens. We'll come up with some sort of ruse to get in. Pretend there is an emergency. A gas leak, or something. Hopefully she'll be a little groggy that early and she'll let us in without a problem."

"She knows who I am so I can't be there for that," Willie said. "I'm definitely in on Sarah."

Tom had a suggestion. "I could wait in my van near Sarah's train station. Once you guys have her in the other van, Hank can come with me and we'll drive to Queens and grab the other one. Darryl and Willie, you guys bring Sarah up here and a few hours later, me and Hank will be on our way with Jennifer."

"That sounds good to me," Darryl said. Hank and Willie nodded in agreement.

"That would be great," Bruce said. "They'll both be here Saturday morning and we can hold the event early Monday morning. That'll give the guests enough time to get here."

"How many people will there be?" Darryl asked.

"We want a small, intimate group. We decided on six. People will be inclined to bid higher. No one wants to be the tenth person into the party with something like this. There might not be anything left to play with," Marilyn said with a chuckle.

"We're going to send out the formal invite tomorrow morning and start taking bids. Guys, we can't thank you enough," Bruce said.

"It's been a lot of work, but it's been enjoyable. We'll get you your girls," Darryl said.

CHAPTER 18

MONDAY JUNE 12, 2017

Ruth Barrett was still grieving the loss of the only man she'd ever loved. Francis, her husband of forty years, had died two weeks earlier from a catastrophic stroke. He was only sixty-two and had otherwise been healthy. He'd been three years away from retiring as the neighborhood dentist of a small town in Pennsylvania.

Ruth didn't work, but she did a lot of volunteering. At sixty years old, she likely had a lot of years left and at this point she had no idea what to do. She felt so alone.

Ruth and Francis had one child together, Angela, who had dropped off her three-year-old son to spend the day with his grandmother. Angela thought it would be helpful for Ruth to have some company, and like any grandmother, she just adored the little boy. When Angela left, Ruth asked him if he wanted to go to the park and play on the swings.

She loved when his face lit up like that.

She held her grandson's hand and they walked to the park. He was very talkative and eager to impress his nana with his knowledge of different objects that he pointed out as they passed them.

Angela was right. This is really helping.

There was only one other mother with her daughter on the swing set when they arrived. The little boy ran to the swings and waited as Ruth followed and tried to keep up. She picked him up and strapped him into the seat. She pushed him and enjoyed his euphoric yelling, but she was distracted by her phone buzzing in her pocket. She took it out and read the text message.

"Log on for details."

She knew exactly what the message meant. She stopped the swing and unbuckled her grandson, much to his dismay.

"Nana has to go home and take care of something, okay? We'll come right back."

The sudden surge of adrenaline allowed her to carry him back to her house. When they got back home, she put him in the playpen and dashed to her computer. She logged in to the encrypted, untraceable message board and clicked on the latest group message.

Hello All:

We hope this message finds you well. We want to thank everyone for your interest and incredible, undying support for this endeavor. We are happy to say that our venue is now fully equipped, and we are ready to proceed!

The event will be held at our home at ***5:00 am EST on Monday, July 17th.*** Please note that this date is tentative and is subject to last minute change. We have two women targeted as our guests of honor for the event.

With this message, bidding for entry into the event is now open. Please review the attached photos and information on the two targets, and submit your bid by next Friday, June 23rd.

The minimum bid is $90,000, and we will take the six highest bidders. Please appreciate the amount of planning, as well as the risk that is involved in acquiring the two women and bid accordingly.

The winners will be notified, and we must be paid in full by Friday, July 7th for you to gain entry into the event. Information about how to wire the money will be provided to the winners.

The women will be kidnapped nearly simultaneously and delivered by the morning of Saturday, July 15th. Once they are in our custody, a message with photo evidence will be sent to the winners.

For those who are not one of the high bidders, portions of the event will be captured on video, and will be available for sale. You will need to message us privately if you are interested in that. Just please be aware that the video will contain a comparatively small part of the event.

If you have any questions, please do not hesitate to ask!

Good luck with your bids! We are looking forward to meeting some of you soon.

Ruth's inheritance would be more than enough, she hoped. Her grandson was entertaining himself in the playpen. She clicked on the first of the two attachments titled "Target #1." There were thirty photos of the woman. She was tall and white, with long black wavy hair. Evidently she had no idea she was being photographed. Her name was Sarah McConnell and she was a veterinarian at an animal hospital in Manhattan. A link led to her biography page on the hospital's website. She was an Ivy League girl.

Underneath the pedigree information was an outline of what they had planned for her. Amazingly, they intended to keep her alive too. Ruth closed her eyes and pictured the outdoor scene. She could imagine the screaming.

Mmm. Sarah. If they can really pull that off, that would be quite a sight.

Next, Ruth clicked on "Target #2". Many of the thirty photos were taken in Manhattan. She clearly worked in the corporate world. Some pictures showed her jogging, which highlighted her athletic, extremely well-toned body. She was much prettier than Sarah.

She's gorgeous. My God.

Her name was Jennifer, and the location of the Manhattan office building where she worked was provided. She was also white, with shoulder length light brown hair. She appeared to be around the same height as Sarah, maybe an inch or two shorter. Jennifer's upcoming ordeal was also briefly summarized, subject to each customer's personal tastes.

Ruth closed her eyes and imagined Jennifer at her mercy. She would have a lot of fun with her for sure. Bruce and Marilyn had described a rather impressive array of tools that would be on hand for the event. Ruth wasn't sure where she would start, but she knew that she wanted to hurt this girl. Badly.

The message contained a link that took her to a page to submit her bid. She would empty her inheritance and savings for this.

She typed in her bid: $145,000

She closed the computer, picked up her grandson and as promised, took him back to the park. She just loved how goofy and happy he always was.

CHAPTER 19

TUESDAY JUNE 27, 2017

"What do you say we make it official?" Sean asked.

"I took myself off the market last week, babe," Sarah replied.

Sarah had taken the train to Manhattan early so that they could meet for lunch. They walked down the block to a Japanese restaurant, but stopped and had their first kiss as a legitimate couple.

"I'm so happy," Sarah said.

"Me too, sweetie."

At the restaurant, they both ordered Sake. When the drinks came, Sarah asked the waiter if he could take a photo of the two of them. He took her phone and snapped a picture as the new happy couple held their glasses together.

"So, do you have any plans for the Fourth?" Sean asked.

"Usually my dad has some kind of party. He loves playing the grill master. The Fourth of July is like, his favorite day of the year. So a few of my friends usually come over for that. You should come."

"I'd love to. Sounds like a blast. I'm taking Monday the third off. I want to get out of town for the weekend. Do you want to come with?"

"Yeah! I'm not sure I can take Monday off, but possibly. Where were you thinking?"

"Somewhere driving distance. A short road trip. Have you ever been out to the Hamptons?"

"No, but I've *always* wanted to go," Sarah said excitedly.

"Then we'll make it happen. I'll look into hotels when I get back up to the office. We'll have that nice walk on the beach one night. We can come back Monday morning if you can't get off work. It's only a two-hour drive or so. And then we'll do your parents' party on Tuesday."

"Sound like a plan. I'm so excited!"

They ate a quick lunch and Sarah walked with Sean back to his office building, then she headed uptown on the subway. She would get to work about an hour early.

Totally worth it. I have a boyfriend!

She updated her Facebook relationship status and received dozens of "likes" within minutes, then she got off the subway, she picked up a cup of coffee and relaxed in the staff lounge. She called her father.

"Hey sweetheart, what's up?"

"Nothing. Just hanging out at the office before my shift. How are you?"

"I'm good. Just wrapped up an appendectomy. Heading to lunch in a bit."

"Cool. Hey, so next Tuesday are you having your Fourth of July get-together?"

"Of course. You're coming, right?"

"Yeah, definitely. So that guy I've been dating, we're official now and it would be a great time for you to meet him so I invited him. That okay?"

"Absolutely. Congrats to the two of you. I'm sure he's a great guy. Looking forward to it."

"He really is. It's been such an amazing year. You two can talk baseball. He's *really* into it. I'm going to invite Allison and her husband too, okay?"

"No problem sweetheart. The more the merrier."

"Do I need to bring anything?"

"No, I'll get everything this weekend. This guy isn't a vegetarian or anything like that is he?"

"Nope, he'll be good with whatever."

Her phone beeped, a message from Sean. She wrapped up the conversation with her father and checked the text message, a link for a hotel in the Hamptons.

"Right on the beach," he texted.

"Perfect :) Can't wait."

"Me neither. Leave early Saturday morning?"

"Yep sounds good!"

"Good. Love you."

"Love you too."

* * *

Jennifer didn't have any meetings for the rest of the day, so she took a minute to pop into her boss' office.

"Hey Jen. What's happening?"

"Oh, not much. I know you're busy but I'm looking to take the week of July twenty-seventh off for vacation. Would that be okay?"

"Fine with me. You going anywhere or is it a stay-cation?"

"Cancun. With my best friend from college."

"Very nice. I've been there a few times. You'll love it. Yeah, just let H-R know."

"Great, thanks so much."

She'd also let her clients know in the coming days and weeks, but first she returned to her office and texted Danielle.

"Good for that week."

"Okay yes!!!!" Danielle responded.

"Booking hotel and flights now."

"Margaritas and beach w/ my love!!! <3 <3"

She had three hours left at work. She pulled out one of her client's files and stared at it. Her mind was already on the beach in Cancun.

* * *

SadisticMistress34: Bill, are you there? Do you have a minute to talk?

Torturer47: Yes, how are you Marilyn?

SadisticMistress34: Very well. Bruce and I have reviewed all the bids, and I am happy to tell you that you are the third highest bidder!

Torturer47: Excellent!! I had my fingers crossed.

SadisticMistress34: Congratulations! The bids were outstanding. The high bid was $155,000, the lowest was $120,000. A lot in the 95-105 range.

Torturer47: Well deserved. The girls look marvelous. Great choices. You'll have my full payment next week.

SadisticMistress34: Terrific. We will keep you updated, and if the date changes we will let you know right away.

Torturer47: No problem. Good plans in place?

SadisticMistress34: We think so. Great crew working for us and they will be compensated accordingly. If all goes as planned, we'll send you a message early on July 15th, and then we're a go for the 17th. Bright and early!

Torturer47: Really looking forward to it. Been a long time coming for me.

SadisticMistress34: Us too. It will be a memorable day. And maybe the first of many events :) Just so you know, the order of turns with Jennifer will be based on the bid amounts. So you'll have her third for 15 minutes and hopefully she'll last long enough so everyone will get quite a few rounds with her. We want to keep her alive as long as possible, so it will be all about pacing yourselves and not getting too overzealous too early in the game. Oh, and make sure you come hungry . . .

Torturer47: I will! Sounds like you guys have thought of everything. Can't wait. How do I wire you the money?

Marilyn gave him the instructions, as she had done with Howard Helton and Ruth Barrett, the two top bidders.

"Just talked to Bill, the professor at Penn State, and let him know he's in. He's going to pay by next week," Marilyn said to Bruce as he arrived home from work.

"Trucking right along."

"Yep. Three more to go and then I'll give Darryl a call. Also, Sarah has a boyfriend now. I checked her Facebook page this afternoon."

"Too bad for them it won't be a long-term relationship," Bruce said amusingly.

Marilyn opened Facebook and showed him the picture of Sarah and her boyfriend in the restaurant.

"She really does look great these days," Bruce said.

"Yes, she does. Looks like she shed a few pounds. Happy, so vibrant and full of life. She's going to be great."

Marilyn was looking forward to giving Darryl and his crew the good news. The six high bids totaled $824,000. Darryl and his team would be paid $618,000.

Tomorrow was June 28th. Only sixteen days away from the abductions.

CHAPTER 20

THURSDAY JULY 13, 2017

Bruce, Marilyn, and the kidnap crew met one final time late in the afternoon. The six guests had paid in full. The four men would each be paid $154,500.

Darryl said, "We're ready to go tomorrow. Me, Hank, and Willie are going to do Sarah. Once she's incapacitated and secured, Hank and Tom will drive to Queens and grab Jennifer. Hank is on double duty."

He continued, "Hank and Tom will pose as gas company workers. They have fake identification cards and we found uniforms online. The key will be getting into her house quickly without causing any sort of scene."

"If there is even a *chance* of a problem, don't go through with it. There will be other opportunities," Marilyn said.

"I don't anticipate problems. We'll have them here before anyone even realizes they are missing," Darryl said.

"Is there anything at all you need from us?" Bruce asked.

"No, we're all set. Thanks for the chloroform and for helping out with Sarah. We have everything else ready to go," Darryl said.

Bruce and Marilyn had offered to watch Sarah's house the next afternoon and confirm that she left for work. Willie would wait outside of the animal hospital in his car and make sure Sarah left at the normal time and got on the subway to head home. Then he would race to Long Island where Darryl and Hank would be waiting in Darryl's van.

Tom's job was to sit in his van outside of Jennifer's house and verify that she came home on Friday night. Then he would drive to Long Island and pick Hank up once Sarah was under control. There were a lot of moving pieces, but they were all optimistic that the plans would go down without a hitch.

"You all planning on hanging out for the show?" Bruce asked.

"We wouldn't miss it. We've been watching these girls for months, and we'd love to see how it all ends for them," Darryl said.

"Great. And the weather for Monday is looking perfect. Guys, good luck tomorrow. Keep us posted and let us know if there are any problems."

* * *

The four men had dinner at a bar and restaurant in Manhattan and talked about what they would do with their money. They had all already left their jobs months ago, and if this went as planned, they wouldn't have to work again for a while.

"They might do this again, you know," Hank said.

The other three agreed they would be interested in any future plans that Bruce and Marilyn had. And the longer they talked the more they learned how little any of them cared about how unspeakable and horrifying it would be for Sarah and Jennifer.

The rape is going to be the easy part, Tom thought to himself.

To Hell with them. They didn't know the women, and it was strictly business. They saw the girls as merchandise and a heck of a payday.

"Make sure you guys rest up tonight. We'll have to be on point with *everything* tomorrow," Darryl said.

CHAPTER 21

FRIDAY JULY 14, 2017

Jennifer's phone alarm woke her at 6:30 a.m. She shut it off and stretched out, and then the migraine hit her.

Fuck.

Her vacation was coming up, so she couldn't take the day off. She forced herself to get out of bed and tried to do some calisthenics but the pain in her head was unbearable. Instead, she brewed a strong cup of coffee and gulped down three extra-strength Tylenol with a glass of water.

Today was the start of a five-day heat wave in the northeast, and she could feel it already. She took a cool shower, thinking it would help the migraine, but it got worse. Through the throbbing pain she thought about the long day of meetings. One of them was with a new potential client, which would involve an avalanche of paperwork and her full, undivided concentration. She felt like crying.

She slowly sipped her coffee while dressing and dreaded the day. She didn't think she couldn't handle the subway commute today so she decided to Uber instead.

Five minutes later the driver honked from outside. She grabbed her phone, her keys, and her purse and walked to the car. She noticed the male driver staring at her legs as she approached.

Not in the fucking mood today.

She got in the back, gave the driver the address of her office building and then closed her eyes. She slowly rubbed her temple with her fingers in a clockwise manner.

It's going to be a long fucking day.

Tears came in her eyes. The pain was agonizing.

* * *

Sarah's alarm woke her at 9:30 a.m. She gave Gizmo a pat and went to the bathroom to look at herself in the mirror. The sunburn from the weekend in the Hamptons and the Fourth of July party had finally settled into a tan.

God damn Irish skin.

She felt even better when she got on the scale. 155 pounds. She wanted to maintain that weight and look good for Sean. With that in mind, she brushed her teeth, put her hair in a ponytail and put some workout clothes on. She was now going to the gym three times a week and she was really into the stair master.

She filled a water bottle and put on her running sneakers.

"Mommy will be right back, bud!"

She spent an hour at the gym and worked up a nice sweat. She got back home, took a cold shower and then made herself a fruit salad. While she ate, she texted her boyfriend.

"Hey! All set for the weekend?"

Sean was going to Atlantic City, New Jersey for a friend's bachelor party.

"Yep leaving right from work. How was the gym?"

Sarah took a selfie of herself flexing a muscle and sent it.

"American Gladiators, I'm coming for you!"

"Lol. You're adorable. I'm coming back early Sunday morning. I come over?"

"Yes please :) We'll stay under the covers and binge on Shameless? Figure we could both use a relaxing day. How's work so far?"

"Slow for now. Hey I was looking at this place in Lynbrook. They do these cooking classes for couples. I thought it would be fun," Sean typed.

"Ummmm, are you trying to say something about my cooking??? ;)"

"Lol, no babe. Just a fun night out. We'll have some laughs. Hey, I've got to go in to a meeting in a few then I'm taking off."

"Okay . . . lame. Anyway, have an awesome trip! Tell everyone I said hey."

"Will do babe, love you."

"Love you too."

Life couldn't be much better. She had a job that she adored and a man that she loved who treated her like a queen. Marriage and children were on the horizon. Sean was the *one.*

She snapped out of her daydream and checked Facebook. She "liked" and commented on a few posts from her close friends and got dressed for work. She wore a light blue tee shirt, blue jeans, and her favorite comfortable pair of grey Converse sneakers.

"Mommy's going to work. Be a good boy!"

Life is so good right now.

* * *

"There she goes."

Bruce and Marilyn watched Sarah McConnell leave her house and get in her car. They followed her as she drove towards the Long Island Rail Road station and parked her car on the usual side street. They continued to tail her as she walked to the station.

When she got on the train, Bruce called Darryl. "She's on her way to work. We're on. See you guys tonight."

Bruce and Marilyn's job was done, and they headed back home.

* * *

Jennifer's last meeting of the day was over, a consultation with a young computer software engineer. The meeting had gone well, and he had hired her to manage his money. Once he left, she shut the door and sank into her chair, closed her eyes and tried to focus on the cool air conditioning. Her head was still pounding, and she chugged half of a bottle of water with two more Tylenol. She slowed her breathing and rubbed her temples. It was just before five o'clock.

I'm out of here.

She requested an Uber, shut her computer off and said her goodbyes as she left the office. By the time she got downstairs and to the street, the car was waiting for her. The aroma of sausages cooking in the nearby corner food cart made her nauseous. The sound of car horns beeping, typical of a Friday rush hour in New York City, were piercing her skull. She got in the car and closed her eyes, hoping to get some sleep on the way home. The driver was heavy on the gas and brakes as he maneuvered between lanes, and Jennifer knew that sleep was impossible.

Still better than the subway.

When she got back home, she kicked off her heels, took her work clothes off and tossed them on the floor in the closet. She'd deal with that tomorrow. She put on a white tank top, turned the air conditioner in her bedroom on full blast, washed up, took three shots of Nyquil and got into bed.

She buried her face into her pillow was out cold in ten minutes.

* * *

"She's home," Tom said to Darryl on the phone.

"Good. You going to hang out there a bit?"

"Yeah, it's a little early. She turned the lights out. Maybe taking a nap or hopefully in for the night."

"Let me know."

"Will do. I'll see you guys tonight."

* * *

Sarah finished an appointment with a dog afflicted with kennel cough and went out for a quick slice of pizza before wrapping up her shift with a phone call, some paperwork, and one more appointment, a routine checkup with a puppy. She checked on the cat that was housed for two nights after undergoing a blood transfusion.

It was just after ten o'clock, and she was clear for the rest of the night. She had to stay in case of any walk-in emergencies, but everything was quiet and she hoped it would stay that way for the rest of the night.

She checked Facebook, then opened the text message thread with Sean. She started to type:

"Hey, how's everything?"

She deleted the text. She wanted to talk to him, but she didn't want to be the girlfriend who hovered, although she was well aware of what often took place during bachelor parties.

Just let him be and let him have his fun with the boys.

She thought he'd check in with her at some point over the weekend but if not, she would see him Sunday morning anyway. The rest of the shift was uneventful. She turned her office computer off and hung up her white lab coat.

"Everyone have a good weekend!" she said to her staff as she left.

As she always did, she took the subway to the Long Island Rail Road. The train was on time, and it was fully air-conditioned which was always a crapshoot. The car she was on was mostly empty and once the conductor checked her pass, she relaxed in her seat and closed her eyes. She spent the last ten minutes of the train ride on Facebook, catching up on what her friends did all day.

She got out of her seat as the train pulled into her station. She and three other people got off and she walked towards the street where her car was parked. As usual, it was quiet outside except for the sounds of crickets chirping. She turned the corner and was about eighty feet from her car.

And now she walked her final steps as a free woman. She never knew that she was the center of the universe to a ravenous group of depraved individuals. She had no idea that she had been watched for months, and that tonight was the night. How could she know? If she knew that she'd never talk to her loved ones again, she would have told them all how much they mattered to her. She would have told her parents that she loved them one more time. She would have spent one more minute with Sean. Just one extra minute and a kiss would have been enough.

She never saw it coming, and she was no match for them.

* * *

Sarah McConnell had been spotted on a Tuesday night in February. After all the work and all the planning during the past several months, it took less than five seconds to kidnap her.

The operation was based on timing. Willie followed her on foot and rushed her from behind as Darryl pulled up alongside of her. Willie zapped her in the neck with a high-voltage stun gun, which momentarily incapacitated her, then bear-hugged her and dragged her to the van. The sliding door was already opened, and Hank—dressed in his blue uniform for Jennifer's abduction—pulled her inside. Willie hopped in and shut the door.

It was scary how *easy* it was.

While Hank kept her under control in the back of the van, Darryl drove to the spot where they would meet Tom. Willie soaked a rag with chloroform and covered her face with it. He straddled her chest and held down one arm, while Hank held the other. Already disoriented from the stun gun, she kicked her legs but didn't put up much of a fight. Her eyes rolled up, and she was out cold in ninety seconds. They had been instructed by Bruce and Marilyn to leave her clothes on.

Darryl pulled over next to Tom's van at the predetermined rendezvous point.

"Good luck brother, be safe out there," Darryl said as Hank got out.

"You too, guys. We'll see you in a few hours," Hank replied.

Darryl drove and Willie stayed in the back. He fished through Sarah's purse and found her iPhone. When he picked it up, it flashed right to the time and the date with the home screen wallpaper in the background. It was a picture of her and her boyfriend—one of those silly selfies with both of them making a funny face. He shattered the phone with a hammer.

He then reached into the tool bag and pulled out a large red ball gag and a stack of zip ties held together with a rubber band. He stuffed the ball gag into the sleeping woman's mouth and secured it tightly in place around the back of her neck. Her neck was damp with sweat.

He took the rubber band off the zip ties, then yanked her sneakers off and rolled her over onto her belly. He secured her ankles and knees together, then placed her arms behind her back and bound her elbows and wrists together so that the palms of her hands touched.

"All good back there?"

"All good. Calling now."

Willie called Bruce and let him know that they had Sarah. They would arrive in about two and a half hours.

"Great work. Take your time and drive safely," he said.

* * *

Her eyelids were heavy. So damn heavy, and she didn't care about anything else. She cared enough for one second to try to open her eyes, but everything was cloudy so she gave up. All she wanted to do was stay sleeping. What was that humming sound though? She was laying on a hard surface, but that sound was pleasant at least. Maybe she would try to wake up in a few minutes. There were bumps every ten or twenty seconds. She didn't really like those.

She wanted to shift her position, but what was that intense pain in her wrists? It felt like her wrists were being bitten. Worse than that, she couldn't move them and they were stuck behind her back. What the hell was going on? She tried to open her eyes again. She faintly heard a man talking. She wanted to talk too, but there was something hard in her mouth. She tried to stand up. Her socks were on, but what happened to her sneakers? And why was that same biting sensation being felt at her ankles? Why were her feet stuck together? Something wasn't right. The humming sound continued, but she couldn't move and she couldn't talk. Her head was absolutely pounding.

Finally, she was able to open her eyes. At first, everything was spinning for a bit but when it stopped, she clearly saw a man with a sinister smile looking down at her. Then, it all came back to her quickly.

* * *

Thirty minutes into the drive, Sarah McConnell woke up. She screamed and struggled, flopping around like a fish out of water. Her eyes darted around and it didn't take long before she was crying ferociously. Willie laughed, enjoying the show as she tried to kick him with her bound ankles.

"You might want to save your energy, sweetheart. You will have *a lot* more to scream about later," Willie said.

While his partner taunted the precious live cargo in the back, Darryl pulled onto the Taconic State Parkway. He stayed to the right and obeyed the speed limit. There wasn't much traffic at all, but a car would occasionally pass on the left. Who knew where they were coming from, or where they were headed?

All that mattered was that their terrified prey was securely bound and gagged in the back of the van and nobody else on the road knew that.

Man, this bitch can cry.

Darryl somehow maintained his focus on the road with an erection that was about to explode.

CHAPTER 22

SATURDAY JULY 15, 2017

Jennifer was at her off-campus apartment a half-mile away from the University of Connecticut. Her family was driving up from New York for her graduation and they were going out for dinner tonight. Suddenly, out of nowhere, it hit her.

Oh Jesus Christ! Fuck!

She completely forgot. She had registered for another class at the start of the semester, but a week later decided that didn't want to take it. She signed up for another one, but forgot to drop the first class. The final exam was today and if she failed the final, she couldn't graduate.

Her heart raced and sweat poured down her face. She still had the textbook, and she tried to cram as much as she could while she rushed to campus.

How the fuck did I let this happen?

A persistent alarm going off from out of nowhere took her mind off the exam for a moment. It got louder and louder . . .

Jennifer snapped awake. It took her a moment to realize that it was just that nightmare again and she was safe in her dark bedroom at her house in Queens. She had been in a deep sleep since the evening before. The doorbell was ringing incessantly and she looked at the time. It was 4:37 a.m. The bell was so loud and she often exaggerated that it sounded like she lived in a fire house. It was the least favorite thing about her home.

Who the fuck is at the door at this time?

The ringing didn't stop, so she put on a pair of black mesh shorts and scampered to the door, turning on the living room light on the way. She unlocked the door but left the chain on and opened the door just a crack. She was greeted by two men wearing matching uniforms and fluorescent vests. One of them was holding a tool bag.

"Good morning, ma'am," the other said. "Sorry to bother you at this hour."

"What is it?" Jennifer asked, squinting her eyes.

They held up identification cards.

"There's been an emergency. A gas leak has been reported on this block and we need to check everyone's gas lines. I'm very sorry for the inconvenience but we'll be out of here in less than a minute if everything checks out. Can we come in?"

"Um, sure. Gas leaks scare the hell out of me. Come in."

"Thank you."

She undid the chain, let the two men in and shut the door. She realized immediately the situation was a lot more serious than a gas leak.

"Don't fucking say a word, okay? Just stay calm and you won't get hurt," one of them said, pointing a gun at her face. She froze, immobilized by fear.

"Do you fucking understand?"

She nodded and watched in terror as the man with the bag opened it and pulled out two zip ties.

"On your knees."

She was frozen in shock and didn't move.

"*Now!*"

"Just don't hurt me, please. Take what you want and leave. I won't tell anyone," Jennifer struggled to say as she got down on her knees.

"Oh, we will take *exactly* what we want. Just do what we say and we won't hurt you. First things first. We're going to tie you up. We've been watching you for a while. We know you live alone and know your parents sometimes come to visit on Saturdays. We also know that we have plenty of time before that happens," he said, while his partner bound her wrists behind her back.

"Face down on the ground," he said, pressing the gun to the back of her head.

She felt rough hands on her ankles and bare feet, then the zip tie tightly binding her, causing her to wince as it was digging painfully into her skin.

"Please don't hurt me," she whimpered.

"Just cooperate. It's the easiest way out for you. Now, honey, where is your cell phone?"

"On the nightstand in the bedroom."

"Atta girl. You got it Hank?"

Hank walked into the bedroom and returned with her cell phone. "Password."

"Nine seven nine, two three two," Jennifer answered. She noticed he was wearing gloves.

"Very good, see how easy this can go?" Hank said, going through her phone. "Sending a text message to Mommy. You need a little weekend getaway by yourself so you're telling Mommy not to stop by this weekend. Okay?" He returned the phone to the bedroom and on the way back retrieved her purse from the dining room table. He pulled out her wallet and took her driver's license.

"Jennifer Miller! It is *so* nice to finally meet you," he said, putting her license in his pocket.

"What are you going to do to me? Please, just take what you need and go. Please," Jennifer said.

"We will. We'll be out of here very shortly. Don't you worry. Your garage, is it manual or is there a remote?"

"There's a remote on top of the garage in the table," she answered.

He laughed.

"You mean on the table, in the garage. It's okay. It's early. We get it."

Her mind raced, and she had a dreadful feeling this was more than a robbery. They were relaxed and everything they did had a purpose. They were too well-prepared. She lay still on floor, the gun pointed at her, and watched as Hank entered the garage through the side door. She heard the garage door hum as it opened.

"We good out there?"

"All good. All quiet," Hank replied .

She heard a vehicle pull into the garage, followed by the sound of the garage door closing.

"We're almost out of here," the gunman said. He rolled her onto her back. "And you're coming with us," he added.

"Please, no!" She started to yell, but was quickly stifled when Hank crammed a rag over her face. It was wet and smelled of a heavy solvent. With her hands and ankles tied, she was completely helpless, but fought with all of her might to break free, realizing that she was being kidnapped. She tried to scream, but dizziness overcame her, and her world faded to black.

* * *

"She out?" Tom asked.

"Yep, she's gone," Hank responded.

Tom put the gun back in his vest pocket. Hank reached into the tool bag and pulled out a large red ball gag.

"She is seriously fucking hot. God damn," Hank said as he inserted and secured the ball gag in her mouth.

"Yeah, she is some catch. She'll have some fight in her too."

"Just the way I like it. Ready? One, two, three."

Tom lifted her legs, and Hank lifted from under her arms. They carried her into the garage and placed her on the floor in the back of the van. Tom got in the driver's seat and Hank returned to the house, turned off the lights and retrieved the tool bag. Tom closed the garage door with the remote as they left. Hank called Bruce.

"Hank," Bruce answered.

"We got her. On our way."

"Perfect. Drive safely, guys. Darryl and Willie should be here with Sarah shortly."

"Great. We'll see you in a couple of hours."

"Hey, did you guys get a look at her ID?"

"Yeah. Jennifer Miller. 28 years old."

"Good. Thanks. Clothes stay on."

"Yep, no problem. We'll see you soon."

It had been a long day and they were tired, but the abduction of Jennifer Miller was executed flawlessly. Hank kept a close eye on her, ready to render her unconscious again if necessary. They didn't have to energy to deal with a terrified, frantically screaming woman.

But she was astonishingly beautiful, and they would certainly take great pleasure in having their fun with her later.

CHAPTER 23

SATURDAY JULY 15, 2017

Darryl pulled the van into the garage just after five in the morning. Bruce and Marilyn waited eagerly as Willie got out and opened the sliding door, revealing a bound, gagged, and unconscious Sarah McConnell. The areas under her eyes were damp.

"She looks so beautiful!" Marilyn said excitedly.

"I had to use the chloroform again about five minutes ago. She's one hell of a crier," Willie said.

"Just lay her out on the dining room table for now," Bruce instructed.

"She's a big girl," Darryl said as they carried her inside of the house.

"Cut the ties, please. Tom and Hank are on the way with Jennifer. They hit the road about twenty minutes before you got here," Bruce said.

"Perfect," Darryl said. He cut the zip ties off, but the red ball gag stayed in her mouth.

Bruce and Marilyn carried the long titanium pole and set it down on the table next to her.

"Just something we need to do really quick for the chef but before that, let's get these fucking clothes off," Bruce said.

Darryl peeled her tee shirt off, while Marilyn removed her socks revealing maroon-colored toenails to match her fingernails. Bruce unbuttoned her jeans, then viciously yanked them off and threw them onto the floor.

"Very nice," Marilyn said as she moaned and slowly ran her hand down Sarah's left leg. Bruce ripped her panties off, revealing a bare *mons pubis*, and Willie unclipped her bra and tossed it to the floor. Four pairs of hands roughly fondled the veterinarian's naked body, taking turns rubbing breasts, thighs, and crudely inserting their fingers into her vagina.

"Fuck yes," Bruce said.

"Very nice body. Very fuckable," Darryl agreed.

"And very suitable for what you have planned for her," Willie said.

"Absolutely. Just bear with me for a second here. We need to take a few pictures of her and mark off this pole, then she's all yours," Bruce said.

Marilyn took a few pictures of Sarah then left to upload them. Bruce stretched her arms out and over her head on the table. He placed her wrists together, and then did the same with her feet. He moved the pole so that it was touching her body, and marked the pole with masking tape, indicating where her ankles, knees, waist, elbows, and wrists were.

"Alright, that's it guys. She's all yours."

Darryl and Willie carried her down the hall into the guest room that had been converted into a holding room. Two king-size beds had been equipped with leather cuffs and a spread-eagle restraint apparatus that ran under each mattress.

The pulley system was installed in the middle of the room, and opposite from the beds were two large 4 x 3 foot dog cages. The room, like the basement, was soundproofed and the door had a padlock installed. A small camera was hooked up in one of the upper corners.

They placed Sarah face-up on the leftmost bed, and secured her wrists and ankles in the leather cuffs. Darryl adjusted the restraints, fully stretching her out. They ran their hands up and down her body, eagerly waiting for her to wake up.

"So, who gets to fuck her first?" Darryl said.

"Coin flip?"

"Call it," Darryl said as he pulled a quarter out of his pocket and flipped it in the air.

"Heads."

The coin landed on the floor and Willie picked it up. "Tails. Lucky bastard."

"Wow, the new decoration looks lovely!" Marilyn joked as she and Bruce walked in.

Suddenly, there was movement on the bed.

"She's waking up." Marilyn said.

The four of them turned their attention to the slowly stirring naked woman on the bed. A few seconds later, she fully regained her bearings and panic set in. Screaming and wailing, she tried to fight out of the cuffs, but could only offer little resistance.

"I've *got* to get a picture of this," Marilyn said.

Willie slid his finger inside her, and Darryl squeezed her breasts while unbuckling his belt, resulting in more high-pitched screams.

"You know what's coming, don't you, baby? I really suggest that you try to enjoy it," Darryl said in a menacing tone as he slid his pants off. Immediately after removing his underwear, he dragged his erect penis across her face.

Marilyn returned with the camera and the two men stepped away from the bed.

"Aw, poor baby," she taunted as she pushed Sarah's hair out of her eyes. Sarah, perhaps hoping to connect with the only other woman in the room, pleaded with her eyes.

"Help? Is that what you're asking for?" Marilyn laughed. "*No one* is coming to help you. *No one* knows that you're here."

Marilyn took a few quick close-ups of Sarah's face. Her tear-soaked, widened eyes looked right into the camera. It was quite the contrast from the happy and quirky extrovert seen in her social media pictures. The flash highlighted the sweat on her forehead and the tears that stained her cheeks. Marilyn smiled as she reviewed the photos.

"*Perfect.* Enjoy her, guys," she said.

Bruce and Marilyn left the room and shut the door. Darryl took the rest of his clothes off and told Willie that it was okay for him to hang around. Sarah grimaced and looked away when she saw Darryl's tremendous erection again.

He got into the bed, his naked body on top of hers. He felt her trembling as he thought about how long they had been watching her without her having the slightest clue. He licked sweat off her neck, reveling in the salty taste of her fear. She screamed when his erect penis traced over her vagina as he moved down, lightly biting her breasts. He closed his eyes, heightening his senses as he soaked in the sounds of her terror and the feel of her quivering body beneath him.

All of that hard work. Now, pure bliss.

He opened his eyes and looked down at her face. It was still going to get even better. She wasn't some scantily clad cock tease who had this coming to her. He knew that she didn't deserve this, and that made it all the hotter to him. She was an Ivy League educated, innocent young woman, unaware of the evil that lurked in the hearts of so many human beings. She was about to get a crash course though. She was beyond terrified, and he didn't feel an ounce of remorse or empathy.

He pushed roughly inside of her, feeling the warmth of her and savoring her agony and distress. As he thrust into her, he focused on her face. She cried and looked away, squeezing her eyes shut. This pissed him off.

"Fucking *look at me!*" he screamed, pulling her hair and forcing her to look straight up into his eyes. Once he had her there, he pressed down on her neck.

Much better.

He had a firm hold, mindful of the pressure on her neck to avoid choking her. He picked up his pace, staring down at her face. He flashed back to a moment months ago. He saw her walking down a street laughing and smiling while texting on her phone. Then he was back in the moment, savagely raping her. The pain on her face fueled his brutal lust.

He was in ecstasy, but slowed when he felt himself getting close. He wanted it to last. Her face was turning red, so he let go of her neck. He looked up at the restraints holding her wrists, at her tightly clenched fists. He focused on her crying again. That sound, he thought, would even make a killer like Albert Fish feel penitence.

But not me.

The battle continued within his mind. His primate side longed to plant the seed right now. The dominant sadist in him demanded he prolong her anguish. Ultimately he crossed the threshold of no return. He looked back up at her fists and savored her body struggling underneath him. Her breasts jiggled as she continued to struggle. One more look at the pain on her face was all he needed. Thrusting violently into her with the goal of finishing the job, his breath became rapid, and his heart felt like it was going to burst out of his chest.

He finally exploded inside of her. He pumped harder, deeper, gradually slowing as his semen emptied into her. His mind and body felt numb as he rested his head on her sweaty chest.

"Fuck yes, baby," he said.

Willie was already naked and erect by the time Darryl got off her. He still had the chloroform-soaked rag that he used to render her unconscious, and he used it to wipe her vagina clean. He tossed the rag on the floor and didn't waste any time climbing on her. Darryl sat on the other bed and watched his partner rape her.

He had a full view of one side of her body now, and watched as she continued to cry hysterically and valiantly try to break free. By the time Willie finished with her, Darryl would be ready for round two. He wondered if she had any fleeting hopes for a miracle of survival.

She has no fucking clue how bad it's going to get for her. No fucking clue.

CHAPTER 24

"JESUS CHRIST, LOOK AT HER," Marilyn said.

"This one alone is worth everyone's price of admission," Bruce added.

Jennifer Miller, unconscious, bound, and gagged was laid out on the dining room table.

"Outstanding work guys. No problems, right?" Bruce asked.

"No issues at all. We kept her out for the whole drive. The other guys in the room with Sarah?" Hank asked.

"Yes. We haven't heard from them in a while so they must be having a hell of a time with her," Marilyn said as she turned her camera back on.

"Ready for the clothes to come off?" Bruce asked while holding the pair of trauma shears.

"Just leave her hands and feet tied. We want her strung up to start," Tom said.

Bruce cut the mesh shorts off, followed by her tank top, panties, and bra. The four of them took a moment to stroke her body from top to bottom. She was in incredible shape, with solid abs and muscular, well-toned legs. Her breasts were smaller than Sarah's but firmer. Marilyn took several pictures of Jennifer and then went to upload them.

Bruce walked down the hall and knocked on the holding room door. After a few seconds, Willie, naked and covered in sweat, opened the door, and Sarah's high-pitched screams spilled into the hall. Although she was still gagged, she was able to scream loudly and the soundproofing was working well. Darryl was fucking Sarah for the third time.

"What's up?" Willie said.

"The other girl is here, want to come look?" Bruce replied.

Willie put his underwear and jeans on and met the rest of the group in the dining room while Darryl stayed behind.

"Wow. *Holy shit,*" Willie said, feasting his eyes on the naked, pristine body of Jennifer Miller.

"Me and Tommy get her first," Hank started to say, before Jennifer's muffled screams cut him off. She struggled and kicked as Hank and Tom attempted to hold her down on the table. Willie jumped in and assisted. Marilyn stopped what she was doing on the computer and came out to watch along with her husband.

They got her under control and stood her on unsteady feet. Her hands were bound behind her, her feet were bound together and she was screaming frantically around the ball gag that packed her mouth.

"*Stop fucking fighting!*" Hank yelled as he punched her squarely in the stomach. She keeled over, and they dragged her down the hall into to the holding room.

"You got yourself a roommate," Willie said to Sarah.

Hank pushed her into the middle of the room, under the pulley. Willie and Tom held her still while Hank lowered the hook and lock and attached it to the zip tie at her wrists. He pulled on the rope, forcing Jennifer into an excruciating position, on her feet and bent over with her arms lifted high up behind her back.

She had a clear view of a woman being raped on a bed. She screamed and cursed, trying to stay focused on escape. Her fight-or-flight instinct kicked in, but she could do neither. She honed in for a moment on the horrifying wails coming from the other woman, knowing that in all likelihood, she was next.

"Smile!" Marilyn said as she snapped a few close-ups of her face.

"Need a little help?" Bruce asked as he pulled on Jennifer's hair, holding her face up for better photos.

"Thank you very much," Marilyn said as she took more pictures. She reviewed the photos and she was satisfied. Unlike Sarah, Jennifer portrayed a tough, defiant front.

For now, anyway.

Marilyn kissed Jennifer on the cheek.

"You're a feisty one, aren't you? It's okay. We'll break you down soon enough. Enjoy her, boys," she said as she began to exit the room.

"Bruce. You have to have your shot with them man," Tom said.

He was hoping for the generous offer. His wife smiled and without saying a word, she nodded her approval, walked out and closed the door behind her. His eyes went back and forth between the two women.

"You want the first crack at her?" Hank asked Bruce as he pointed to Jennifer.

"No, you guys break her in. You deserve it. I'll take Sarah when Darryl finishes up with her."

Hank, Tom, Willie, and Bruce took their clothes off just as Darryl finished with Sarah once again and got out of bed. Sarah now had a clear view of Jennifer. The two women who had been watched separately for months briefly made eye contact with each other for the first time. Sarah's view was quickly obstructed once again when Bruce climbed on top of her. He looked down hungrily, licked his lips, and let out a long moan when he put himself inside of her.

At long last, it was his turn.

"God *damn*, girl," Darryl said as he approached Jennifer. While Bruce violently raped Sarah, the four men of the kidnap team circled Jennifer like hawks, groping and exploring every inch of her body. For the first time, Jennifer appeared extremely frightened and she really started to scream. The sounds of the two hysterical women were better than any of the men could have imagined.

It was decided that since Hank had helped with both kidnappings, he'd have the first go at Jennifer. It was only fair. He approached her from behind and wrapped his arms around her, allowing him the leverage to fuck her from behind.

Jennifer was now crying.

* * *

Marilyn read the message that she would be sending to the auction winners one more time:

> Hello Everyone:
>
> I am happy to announce that both women have been successfully abducted, and are being held in preparation for Monday. Please see the attached photos of Sarah McConnell and Jennifer Miller!
>
> We assure you, they are terrified and completely unaware of their individual fates. For your information, Sarah is 30 years old and Jennifer is 28.
>
> We will begin promptly at 5:00 am on Monday so please come on time. We will provide refreshments and light snacks throughout the day before the cookout is complete.
>
> There is no formal attire required. A very hot day is forecast, so please feel free to dress comfortably. You are all also invited to spend the night. We have the space to accommodate everyone.

Travel safely, and we are looking forward to meeting all of you!

-Marilyn and Bruce

She uploaded photos of each woman, naked and laid out on the dining room table, as well as close-ups of their faces when they were awake, then sent the message. She followed that with a separate message to Chris with photos of Sarah's naked body. He had asked for those ahead of time so he could brainstorm ideas for Monday.

She went back to the dining room. The sun was up, and it was a beautiful Saturday morning. Bruce, now back with her after raping both women and cleaning himself up, was affixing the crossbars to the metal pole with cooking twine where he had marked it with the tape.

"How's it coming along?" Marilyn asked as she wrapped her arms around her husband.

"Pretty good, just want to make sure it's nice and tight on there. Seems okay, right?"

Marilyn quickly inspected it with a tug.

"Seems good to me. I'm going to try and get a couple of hours of sleep. You're okay out here?"

"Sure. I'll do another one then head to bed. I hit a wall myself after doing the girls. It was better and more exhausting than I thought. What a day."

* * *

In the holding room, the brutal rape continued with the kidnap team switching up on the two victims. Sarah appeared to be completely out of stamina, as her struggling had all but stopped completely. She lay helpless and spread-eagle on her back, piss and blood from her vagina staining the white sheets.

Jennifer still had fight in her, and struggled through the repeated rapes from behind in that unbearably painful position.

And we're not even halfway done, Tom said to himself.

After the latest round, they decided to give the women a short break. Hank went into the kitchen and returned with four bottles of beer and the trauma shears. Fortified with Viagra, the men toasted and quenched their thirsts, taking in the sights and sounds of what they never imagined could be a reality.

Before they resumed, Willie wiped the semen and blood away from Sarah's vagina. The four men surrounded Jennifer. Two of them held her still while Hank cut the zip tie holding her wrists together. They held her by the arms and dragged her to the empty, clean bed next to Sarah.

"We're equal opportunity here," Willie joked.

They threw her down onto the bed face-up and wrestled her wrists into the leather cuffs. Hank cut the zip tie at her feet, and they cuffed her ankles, leaving her spread-eagle on the bed. Darryl pulled on the strap, completely stretching her out.

Then they uncuffed Sarah's ankles and wrists from the bed, bound her feet together with rope and cuffed her wrists behind her back. They dragged her to the center of the room and hoisted her up with the pulley. Sarah was about to get it from behind.

They raped the women continually and viciously, well into the afternoon, and savored every moment

CHAPTER 25

"WE'RE GOING TO HEAD HOME, wash up, and get some fucking sleep. Holy shit," Darryl said to Bruce and Marilyn.

They laughed.

"Just so you know, we put them in the cages," Willie said.

"Are they gagged?" Marilyn asked.

"Yeah. Gagged, cuffed, and shackled," Tom replied.

"We'll see you guys early Monday morning and help you get the girls set up. Three-thirty or so okay?" Darryl asked.

"Yeah that'll work," Bruce said. "Get some rest, boys."

"We'll keep an eye on the news too. Any problems we'll reach out."

After they left, Marilyn filled two bowls with water while Bruce went down to the basement. He returned with a cattle prod, and they went to check on the women.

"Enjoying your stay, ladies?" Marilyn said.

Sarah was lying on her side sobbing, while Jennifer kicked at the door of the cage. Sarah sat up in the cage and pleaded through the gag.

"Do you have something to say, sweetheart?" Marilyn set the two bowls of water down on a table. Bruce handed her the cattle prod and unlocked Sarah's cage.

"Now just be a good girl and I won't have to use this," Marilyn said while pressing the button on the prod, resulting in a horrifying clicking noise.

"No fucking screaming, do you understand?" Bruce reached into the cage and removed the ball gag from her mouth.

"Please let us go! Please!" Sarah begged.

"C'mon now, you know we can't do that," Bruce said as he took one of the bowls of water.

"Are you going to kill us?" Sarah asked before bursting into tears.

"Why kill the suspense? We do have big, *really big* plans for you. The two of you have made us a lot of money, but I don't want to spoil the surprise," Bruce said.

"*Please,* don't do this. Please. I have a family," she pleaded tearfully.

"You want to drink or not? This is your chance." He held the bowl to her mouth and poured it slowly. Most of it spilled down her chest but she did drink a little bit.

"You especially, you should keep hydrated," Bruce taunted before gagging her again. He shoved her back in and locked the cage.

"Now *this one* might be a bit of a problem," Bruce said as they approached Jennifer.

She sat still while Bruce unlocked the cage. When he opened the door, she tried to lunge out and kick them. Marilyn touched the tip of the cattle prod to Jennifer's belly and zapped her, causing a loud screech and immediate compliance.

Bruce wrestled her back into the cage and removed the ball gag.

"Let us fucking go!" Jennifer screamed.

Bruce held the bowl of water to her mouth, but she jerked and kicked, knocking the bowl out of his hand.

"Fucking *let us go!*"

"Oh well, suit yourself," Bruce said.

Marilyn zapped her again and Bruce put the ball gag back in her mouth.

"All a fucking act. You're no fucking superhero," Bruce said, locking the cage.

"We'll be back to check up on you two. You can scream all you want, the room is soundproofed and the nearest neighbor is half a mile away. Take our advice and just accept your new circumstances. It'll be so much easier on you," Marilyn said.

"Or just keep screaming and fighting. Doesn't matter to us," Bruce added.

They padlocked the door and left the two women in their cages. Marilyn opened the laptop and patched into the holding room camera to monitor the women.

"Okay, I'm going shopping. Let me know if anything comes up," Bruce said as he grabbed the grocery list.

"Will do. I'll be fine here," Marilyn said.

She searched Google for any news on the girls, but found nothing. She'd keep checking every hour or so for the rest of the weekend. She wondered how soon the news would break, and if the police or the media would ever connect the two of them, since they had disappeared about the same time.

Two different jurisdictions. Probably not. Either way, they'll be long gone.

She watched the two women on the computer screen fidgeting with the locks on the cages. Quite entertaining, considering their hands were cuffed behind their backs. She knew they were desperate, but unfortunately for them, there was absolutely no escape.

* * *

Sean decided to check in with Sarah to see if they were still on for tomorrow morning. He'd texted her early that morning but she didn't respond, so he thought he'd give her a call this time. He scrolled down his phone until "Sarah" was highlighted on the screen and hit the call button.

"Hey, you've reached Sarah McConnell. I'm not available at the moment, but please leave a message and I'll call you back as soon as possible. Thanks!"

"Hey sweetheart, just saying hi from Atlantic City. I just had lunch with the guys and we're having fun, even won a few hundred bucks. Anyway, hope you're enjoying your Saturday. Shoot me a text later. Love you."

Her phone rarely went straight to voicemail. Sean guessed that she was probably at the movies, or in the shower. He smiled at that thought.

He got into a taxi with his friends. They were on their way to another casino.

* * *

Marilyn's phone rang. It was Chris.

"Marilyn, how are you?"

"Very good, just finishing setting up for Monday."

"Great. Thanks for sending the photos of Sarah. She really has a great body for this. I have some ideas and I'm on my way to do a little shopping for a couple more things that I need. Do you folks need me to pick anything up?"

"No, we're set. Bruce is actually shopping right now for the refreshments."

"Out of curiosity, did you guys put up a canopy over the pit?"

"Yes, we did! Fifty feet long. It looks great. We also bought a table big enough to seat everyone."

"Very good. Looking forward to seeing it. If you guys could do me one favor, it would be helpful if you can shave any hair off her body."

"No problem. The hair on her head too?"

"I'd lean towards yes, but it's not completely necessary. My concern would be her hair catching fire, but I'll be using charcoal briquettes for the fire. They don't emit any smoke and it'll allow me to keep the heat low and the flames under control. The goal for both of us is very slow cooking, yes?"

"Yes. Absolutely."

"Right. So, I think it's okay to leave the hair on her head. Maybe just tie it into a bun."

"Okay. And we'll give her body a good shave when we clean her up."

"That would help a lot. Thanks a lot. One more thing I wanted to mention. I noticed that her nails have polish on them. Not sure if any of your customers would want to nibble on hands and feet but they wouldn't be able to if the polish stays. Chemicals, toxins and shit. Up to you."

"Oh, that's easy. I'll remove it all when we get her cleaned and prepped."

"Thanks again. No news about them so far."

"Yeah, nothing yet. I've been keeping tabs too. That was one reason why the weekend worked so well, since they wouldn't be missed at work until Monday."

"Well it was a lot of hard work and I'm impressed, and so looking forward to Monday. I'll see you guys around three in the morning."

"Great. See you then. Safe travels!"

* * *

SUNDAY JULY 16, 2017

"Hey, you've reached Sarah McConnell. I'm not available at the moment, but please leave a message and I'll call you back as soon as possible. Thanks!"

Straight to voicemail again.

What the fuck? Did she lose her phone?

Sean had just arrived back in New York City. When he got back to his apartment he checked her Facebook page. She hadn't posted all weekend, which wasn't unusual, but he'd been hoping for some kind of message on her timeline that she'd lost her phone. He dialed her again, and once again it went right to voicemail.

"Hey Sarah, not sure if you're getting these but I hope everything is okay. Give me a call back when you can. Love you."

He took his phone into the bathroom and left it on the sink while he took a shower, hoping that she would call back. The phone stayed silent.

Something isn't right.

He tried calling one more time after his shower. He got dressed, got in his car and headed to Long Island.

CHAPTER 26

SARAH HAD NO CONCEPT OF TIME. Her body had finally given in to exhaustion, and she had even slept for a bit. She had no idea for how long. Unfortunately, this wasn't a nightmare and when she woke up, she was still restrained and gagged in a cage. This was hell. Her cage smelt like urine. Her whole body was sore, but especially her jaw, her wrists, her ankles, and of course her vagina.

She had to go again, so she rolled over to the edge of the cage and peed on the floor. There was still a little bit of blood in the urine. The woman in the other cage turned her back to give her privacy. When she finished, Sarah rolled to the other side of the cage away from the puddle. She had a splitting, shattering headache and her throat was sore from screaming. She might have lost her voice.

She started to cry again as her mind raced with crazy thoughts. She wondered what was going to happen to her. Four of the monsters that had raped her hadn't been seen again and at least a day had gone by. She had been confined in the cage since then, and nothing else had happened yet.

They said they had really big plans for us.

She was terrified of them hurting her, or even worse, killing her. That couple hadn't said a word since the first time they'd given her the water. Every few hours they came back with more water, but they didn't speak. The woman in the other cage seemed defeated now. She'd appeared to be strong at first, physically and mentally, but she was now curled up on her side and sobbing.

The cage was locked. The room's door was padlocked. The situation was hopeless. Sarah's thoughts turned to her family. She wondered what her Mom and Dad were doing and if they knew she was missing or kidnapped. She longed to be safe in her father's arms. She remembered how, when she was a little girl and something bad happened, her mother would always tell her everything would be okay, that it all would work out for the best. Now she longed for the time when that might've been true.

She thought about Sean, and suddenly remembered that she was supposed to meet him. Realistically, he was her only hope.

He knows that I wouldn't just disappear off the face of the earth. He'll call the police.

She thought about the abduction. She tried to remember exactly where she'd been, if there were street cameras on that block.

But how would they know to look there?

She snapped back to the present when the door to the room rattled, and the couple came back in with more bowls of water. The woman held the cattle prod again.

"Wow, it stinks in here," the man said.

"Yeah, it does. Luckily it's almost time to clean you girls up," the woman said.

They unlocked her cage first and removed her ball gag. Sarah was very thirsty.

"Please tell us what you want," Sarah said, her voice badly hoarse.

"Drink up," he said while holding the bowl to her lips. Sarah gulped the cold water down. The man locked the cage again without putting the gag back into her mouth.

They repeated the process with the other girl.

"Please let us go. Please," the other girl begged. They ignored her, but she drank the water compliantly and without fighting. They locked the cage and left her ungagged as well.

"Only a few hours before we start getting you girls ready. We thought you two might want to have a little girl talk before you're separated," the woman said.

"Oh and by the way," the man added on their way out, "no news anywhere about your disappearances. Tootles, ladies."

* * *

Sean drove to Sarah's house and rang the bell. No answer. The lights inside of the house were off. He looked around and didn't see her car either. That made him feel a little bit more at ease. He thought that maybe she'd left for a weekend getaway and forgot her phone.

But she didn't seem stressed or anything.

He tried calling her again, then rang the doorbell again and banged on the door. He stood in front of her house and looked around, trying to figure out what to do next.

* * *

"Have you heard from Jen?" Jennifer's mother asked her husband.

"Nope. I'm sure she's fine. You know she likes to do her own thing," he responded.

"I know. Just a little weird that she'd text at that hour and not say anything else."

"She likes getting out of the city and seeing new places and doing things spur of the moment. She just needs some peace and quiet. We'll hear from her when she gets home."

She texted her daughter anyway.

"How's the trip? Give us a call when you can."

* * *

"What's your name?"

"Sarah," she replied. What's yours?"

"Jennifer. Listen, whatever happens we have to stay strong, okay? We have to keep fighting and we must keep hoping that someone will find us somehow. We owe it to our loved ones to stay strong."

"What are they going to do to us?" Sarah asked.

"I don't know. You heard what they said about us making them a lot of money? The only thing I could think of is holding us for ransom or human trafficking."

"Oh my *God.*"

"I know. Listen, try to keep calm. We have to focus and pay attention in case they slip up, okay?"

"What do you mean human trafficking? Like sex slaves?"

"I guess. But listen, if that's what they're going to do then they'll keep us alive. They said we're going to be separated, but we *must* stay strong and fight. We'll have people looking for us soon."

"Oh my God, this isn't happening!"

"Look, they came right to my house in fucking *New York City*. Someone had to see something and when the police are called they'll find *something* on a camera somewhere. We have to hope."

"Jesus. They got me right off the street in Long Island. I was just thinking about cameras too but I don't know how they would know where to look."

"They'll backtrack your steps. Is there anyone you know that might have called the police by now?"

"My boyfriend was supposed to come over early Sunday morning. He has to know something is wrong, but I don't know if he would go to the police."

"Those monsters used my phone and texted my mother. They told her I was going away for the weekend."

"Jesus Christ, Jennifer."

"I know. Listen, I'm scared too. I'm *terrified*. But we have to stay strong and focus. Promise me that wherever you are you'll keep fighting, okay? We might get separated, and if we do, I will owe it to you to keep fighting. You have to fight for me too. Don't *ever* stop fighting."

"I will, I promise."

"How long have you been with your boyfriend?"

"Our first date was in May. May sixth actually."

"What does he do?"

"He's a financial lawyer in Manhattan."

"Oh really? I'm a financial advisor in Manhattan. In Midtown."

"I worked in Manhattan too. I'm a vet in an animal hospital on the upper east side."

"You *work* in Manhattan, and so do I. We are getting out of this, okay? We have to keep that mindset."

"I know, sorry."

"They'll find us, Sarah. A lot of people will be looking for us. Then we'll all go out for drinks in Manhattan and get drunk as hell. *Positive* thoughts. People looking for us are going to find us. We're getting out of this."

* * *

Sean didn't want to alarm her parents unnecessarily, but he didn't know what else to do. He remembered where they lived from the Fourth of July party. He drove to their house, but nobody was home and he didn't have their phone number. He waited for them all day and periodically called Sarah's phone.

It was dark when they finally arrived home. Sean got out of his car to meet them.

"Hey, Sean! What are you doing out here?"

"Hey, Mr. McConnell. Have either of you heard from Sarah? Her phone has been going straight to voicemail all weekend. She's not home either and her car isn't in front of her house."

"No, we haven't. We've been upstate all weekend at a friend's place."

Sarah's father called her on his phone. "Hmm. Straight to voicemail."

"I don't know. Something doesn't seem right. Would she just take off without telling anyone?" Sean asked.

"No, that's not like her. Honey, do you want to stay here? Sean and I will take a drive over to Sarah's."

"Do you have a house key?"

"Yeah, let me run inside and get it. Honey, if you hear from her give me a call, okay?"

Sean got into the car with Sarah's father and they drove to her house. They entered the house and were greeted by Gizmo.

"Sarah? Are you home?" her father yelled. There was no answer.

All of the lights were off, and everything seemed undisturbed. The cat's litter box was full and his food and water bowls were empty. That was a red flag for them.

"She treats this cat like a child," Sean said. "Something is wrong. We should go to the police station," he said.

"Jesus Christ. That other girl that went missing lives right around here too," Sarah's father recalled. "I don't think they ever found her."

Sean left food and water for the cat, then they drove to the nearest Nassau County police station. Mr. McConnell called his wife to keep her informed, and instructed her to start calling friends and family to see if anyone had heard anything from Sarah.

"And if you hear from her let us know right away. We're going to the police station now."

* * *

Howard Helton was in bed, wide awake and staring up at the ceiling. He would be on the road at 1:30 a.m. but he still had a few hours to go. His heart raced, thinking about what was going to transpire up in the Hudson Valley.

Fuck it, I can't sleep.

He got out of bed and dressed so that he could take a walk and get a cup of coffee. He nodded to the doorman as he held the door open. It was a hot, steamy Sunday night in New York City. He walked down the street and passed all kinds of people, young and old, all so blissfully unaware of what he would be taking part in later. A young woman jogged towards him and he remembered the pictures of Jennifer while she was jogging. He got a good look at the woman as she ran past him.

She would be good, but Jennifer is so much better.

He bought his coffee from Starbucks and went back up to his apartment. He took his pants and underwear off, logged into his computer and navigated to the recent photos sent by Marilyn.

He jerked off while staring at a naked and unconscious Jennifer Miller on a table. Her body was impeccable. Her skin was unblemished. He was the high bidder, and he would get the first shot with her.

He had no idea what he would do to her first. But the fun was figuring it out.

I'm coming for you very soon. You'll be begging to die when I'm through with you.

* * *

They walked into the police station, right past Jackie Nixon's missing person flier.

"Can I help you, sir?" A female officer asked.

"My daughter. She's missing. We need to talk to someone right now."

"Okay, let's slow it down a second. When was the last time you talked to her?"

"Listen, the same fucking people who took that girl have my daughter now, okay?" Sarah's father yelled, pointing at the flier.

Sean patted him on the shoulder to try and calm him down while the officer got on the phone. A minute later, a detective in a suit introduced himself.

"Detective Frasier," he said extending his hand.

"Jim McConnell."

"Sean Stevens."

The detective walked the two men into his office and sat them down opposite his desk. He took a notepad and pen.

"Okay sir, what's your daughter's name and date of birth?"

"Sarah McConnell. April nineteen, 1987."

"And Mr. Stevens, your relationship?"

"I'm her boyfriend."

"And when was the last time either of you saw her or spoke with her?"

Detective Frasier recorded all the preliminary information on Sarah McConnell. He had her home address as well as her work address, her cell phone number, and the general story as to when anyone had last heard from her.

"You're absolutely positive that she wouldn't just take off on her own, right?"

"Absolutely positive. She's a happy young woman, happy with her life and her career," her father said.

"No mental illness at all, right?"

"None whatsoever."

"Alright. We're going to take a ride over to her house. I'll have an evidence collection team meet us there and we'll take it from there. In light of the circumstances with the other missing girl, we'll treat this as suspicious for now. We'll send other units to the animal hospital in Manhattan tomorrow morning to talk with the employees. In the meantime, we'll also canvass all the hospitals around here. She could have been hit by a car, who knows? But we're going to cover everything."

* * *

MONDAY JULY 17, 2017

Sarah woke up in the dark room. She couldn't figure out how long her hands had been cuffed behind her back. The size of the cage did not allow her to stretch out either, and it was unbearable. She looked over towards Jennifer. She was lying completely still, and Sarah heard some light snoring.

"Jennifer?" she whispered.

No answer. She didn't want to wake her up, but talking to her was helping her stay sane. Sarah was so mentally drained that she was almost calm now. She couldn't guess what was going to happen, but Jennifer gave her some hope. It was the only thing that kept her from losing her mind.

There are people looking for us.

Her eyelids were heavy and she felt like passing out again from exhaustion. The door burst open, jolting her back to attention and waking Jennifer.

The lights turned on, and the four monsters that had raped her entered the room along with the couple. Behind them was another man that they hadn't seen before.

"Oh, my *God, no!*" Sarah screamed.

"It's time, ladies," one of the men said.

"Her first," the woman said, pointing at Sarah.

The four men approached the cage.

"No! Get away from me!"

They pulled her out of the cage and crammed a large ball gag into her mouth. As they dragged her out of the room kicking and screaming, she made eye contact with Jennifer who wascrying hysterically in the cage.

Stay strong and fight. We'll get out of this somehow.

CHAPTER 27

BRUCE AND MARILYN HEADED TOWARDS the basement. Behind them, Darryl and Hank had control of Sarah who fought frantically. The other three men stayed nearby to provide assistance if needed. The men carefully carried her down the stairs, but when she saw the basement, she screamed around her gag and intensified her efforts to get away.

They threw her onto the floor and dragged her to the center of the room. Bruce lowered the pulley apparatus as Darryl uncuffed Sarah's feet and wrestled her ankles into the leather cuffs attached to the spreader bar. Once they were secured, Bruce pulled on the rope and slowly hoisted Sarah up by her ankles with her hands still cuffed behind her back. The hoist was locked in place.

"You all good for now?" Darryl asked.

"Yep, all set. Thanks guys. We'll get you when we're ready for the other one," Bruce replied.

Darryl and his crew left the basement. Chris stayed behind with Bruce and Marilyn. The three of them laughed at Sarah's efforts to break free. Her face was bright red from screaming and the blood rushing to her head.

"A little easier than your niece, I presume?" Marilyn asked.

Chris laughed. "Definitely. This one won't be an issue for me. She'll be a lot of fun and I'm very excited."

"We still need to shave her and take care of the nail polish. It won't take long. We figured we'd wait until the last possible moment," Marilyn said as she tied Sarah's sweaty hair up in a bun.

"No problem. She really is perfect. You guys good down here? I need to start getting the charcoal in the pit."

"Yeah, I think we're good with her. If you need any help get one of the other guys," Bruce said.

"Will do. I'll help you tie her down when she's ready," Chris said before he left.

The large table with the restraints in the middle of the room was positioned horizontally. The long titanium pole, now fully equipped with the five crossbars lay on top of it. A few feet away to the left was another long table, it's contents covered with a black sheet. Six chairs were positioned in a neat semi-circle about twenty feet from the restraint table. In between the third and fourth chairs was a video camera set on a tripod.

All of that was for later. For now, Bruce and Marilyn had to prep Sarah. They decided to get the unpleasant part out of the way first. Bruce laid a tarp out on the floor underneath Sarah. They each put latex gloves and paper facemasks on, and Bruce took an enema kit out of the closet. Marilyn slid a plastic container behind the hanging victim. They nodded to each other, and Bruce slowly inserted the enema tube into Sarah's rectum, resulting in roaring screams.

"I know, I know. Can't have you pissing or shitting while you're cooking though," Bruce said.

She let out another horrified screech. Bruce wondered if that was in response to the word "cooking", or to the physical pain from the tube. Probably both. He squeezed the enema bag, emptying the liquid into her rectum, then pulled the tube out. Marilyn held the plastic container close to her anus, and within a minute her bowels rapidly evacuated. Most of it fell into the container, but some slid down her back and onto her hands.

Bruce refilled the enema bag and cleaned her out a second time. Marilyn took the plastic container filled with human waste out of the basement and flushed it down a toilet in a bathroom next to the holding room. While she did that, Bruce hosed her down with cold water.

"That wasn't so bad, now was it?" he taunted her as Marilyn returned and shut the door.

"It's almost four o'clock. When I'm done shaving her I'll get dressed and get ready to start letting the guests in," Marilyn said.

"Send Chris down when you go up," he said.

Marilyn took a straight razor and held it up against Sarah's right ankle. "Be a good girl and stay still now, I don't want to cut you."

Bruce did his best to hold the frantically crying victim still as Marilyn ran the razor down her right leg. The sharp blade gave a nice, close shave, and she finished the entire leg before moving on to the left. Over the next fifteen minutes, she swiftly and efficiently removed as much hair from Sarah's body as possible.

"There we are, sweetheart. All done! Nice and fresh," Marilyn said.

Marilyn went upstairs and Bruce hosed down Sarah's body again, then dried it off with a towel. Marilyn returned shortly with Chris, a bottle of chloroform, and another camera.

"Okay Chris, we're about all set. The pit ready?"

"Yes sir. Love what you did with the canopy. It looks great out there."

Marilyn snapped her fingers in front of Sarah's face.

"Honey, I want to show you something before we put you back to sleep."

Bruce soaked a rag with chloroform while Marilyn pulled up the photos of Jackie Nixon in the basement. She held the camera in front of Sarah's face and clicked through the photos, first showing a close-up of Jackie's face, and then a few photos of her slaughtered carcass.

Sarah was overwrought.

"And I am happy to say that she had it much easier than you'll have. You will put on a spectacular show, my dear," Marilyn said.

Bruce rendered Sarah unconscious with the chloroform. After all the hysterics, it was eerily quiet as her comatose body hung in silence. Bruce undid the cuffs on Sarah's wrists and let her arms fall. Chris placed a large roll of cooking twine on the table next to the newly constructed rotisserie, and Marilyn had a bottle of non-acetone nail polish remover ready to go with a package of cotton balls. As Bruce lowered her down, Chris guided her body squarely onto the apparatus. The top of the device with the top two crossbars extended off the table. Bruce released the ankles from the leather cuffs letting her feet fall onto the table.

Marilyn gave the two men a quick tutorial and before long, the three of them had removed the polish from her fingernails and toenails. Once they were cleaned and dried, Chris aligned her wrists with the top cross bar.

Using the cooking twine, Chris tightly bound the Ivy League veterinarian's wrists to the pole and cross bar. He used much more than he needed, but he wanted to guard against the disaster of her breaking out of the bondage and falling into the pit. He didn't want to be embarrassed and the attendees had paid a lot of money to be here. He gave her wrists a hard tug and pull, finally satisfied that she couldn't break free.

"The guests will be here soon. I need to get ready. Are you two good down here?" Marilyn asked.

"All good, honey."

"I'll let the guys know that we're almost ready for Jennifer," she said on her way out.

Bruce held Sarah's elbows together while Chris tied them securely to the pole and crossbar. They slid the bottom part of the roasting device with her legs off the edge of the table, and Chris tied her feet and knees down to the bottom cross bars. He checked each of the bonds one more time.

"You'll gag her with something else, right?" Chris asked.

"Yeah, I figured a rag or two and we can seal it in with the twine."

"That works." Chris said as they slid the apparatus back again so that her head was off the table.

Bruce removed the ball gag and shoved two rags into her mouth, packing it well with the top rag partially sticking out. Chris looped cooking twine around the back of her neck, securing her head to the pole as well as the rags in her mouth.

Bruce never appreciated the walkout basement more than this moment. He opened the door leading to the back yard.

"On three?" he said to Chris.

"One, two, three."

They each lifted one end of the apparatus and carried Sarah outside to the barbecue pit, placing the ends of the device into the grooves that had been cut out of the cinder blocks. They took a moment to catch their breath. Chris fastened a metal crank to the end of the pole close to her wrists, then went back inside to retrieve the cooking twine. He stepped into the pit through the open side and tied Sarah's waist securely to the final cross bar in the middle.

"She's not breaking out of that," Bruce said as he gave his own examination.

Chris walked over to the crank.

"Want to do the honors?" he asked Bruce.

Bruce took hold of the crank and gave it one test turn, rotating Sarah a full 360 degrees.

"Perfect," he said.

"Yeah, we'll be doing a lot of that for the next twelve to fifteen hours or so. A lot of turning and a lot of basting," Chris said.

"You'll have plenty of help, I'm sure. It's all about putting on a great show, so just keep her alive for as long as possible."

CHAPTER 28

THE EVIDENCE COLLECTION TEAM was still combing through Sarah McConnell's house, but nothing was turning up. Detective Frasier was back at the stationhouse updating the commanding officer and all supervisors still on duty at this late hour.

"She's a possible missing person. No mental problems, not suicidal. As far as we know, the last time she was seen was Friday night at her workplace. Roberts will go to Manhattan, talk to the staff. The boyfriend says she commutes to and from Manhattan via train, so we'll work with NYPD to pull any video footage around the hospital. We'll see if we can follow her steps that night."

"Any connection to Jackie Nixon at this point?" one of the supervisors asked.

"Not that we know of, other than the fact that Nixon resided about twenty minutes away from McConnell," Detective Frasier responded.

"Any press?"

"Not yet. Keeping them out until we have a little more information. Probably middle of the day."

"Nothing as far as suspects? Witnesses?"

"None as of now. But as I said, we'll be speaking with the staff at the hospital, and Givens is with the family getting friends' names and information. I'm working on retrieving her phone records from Verizon."

"Alright, everyone. We're all putting our personal lives aside. In all likelihood, we have a serial kidnapper in our neighborhood. Turn over every fucking stone until we find these women and whoever is responsible for this. Frasier, you're the lead on this?" the commanding officer asked.

"Yes sir."

"I want updates every hour. Get to work, gentlemen."

* * *

Ruth made the final right turn and found herself on a long winding road in upstate New York. The clock in her car read 4:39 a.m. She hadn't seen another house in quite a while. She flashed her high beams with each turn, finally approaching a large house on the right. The lights on the first floor were on.

This must be it.

She checked her mirrors for traffic around her then pulled onto the property, the headlights illuminating a woman dressed in semi-formal attire. She stopped her car as the woman approached the driver's side with a smile.

"Good morning, can I help you?" she asked.

"Ruth Barrett here for the gathering," she replied with the code phrase.

"Ruth! So nice to meet you, dear. I'm Marilyn. Just pull onto the grass on the right over there. You'll be out of view," Marilyn said.

"Thank you."

Ruth did as she was told and parked her car. Marilyn waited and then they walked in through the front door together.

"Okay, we're waiting for one more," Marilyn announced.

Ruth was introduced to the group gathered in the living room. Bruce, Chris, Darryl, Willie, Tom, and Hank, and the four other guests who had arrived before her; Howard, Bill, Greg, and Michael.

"Would you like wine or coffee?" Marilyn asked Ruth.

"I'll take a glass of wine, thank you," Ruth said, cutting half of a pastry from a tray on the coffee table and putting it on a paper plate.

Marilyn returned with the glass of wine and went back outside. A nervous excitement buzzed in the room as everyone anxiously waited for the event to start. Bill informed Ruth that they would start off with Sarah McConnell, and then do Jennifer Miller who was currently being held in the basement.

"That young woman is just gorgeous, isn't she?" Ruth said to Bill as she took a bite of the pastry.

"Jennifer, right? God, I know. I can't wait to get my hands on her. When do you go up?"

"I'm second, I think," Ruth responded.

"Well I'm right behind you then. Any idea what you'll do to her first?"

"Not particularly, no. I want to see what kind of tools they have. I'll make up my mind then."

"I can't believe this was put together. I really can't. I keep pinching myself," Bill said as he laughed.

Everyone's attention turned to the front door as Marilyn walked in with the final guest at 4:45. Introductions were made and he was asked if he wanted wine or coffee. He declined the offer and sat down. It was almost time to get started.

* * *

Jennifer couldn't move; she was trapped in complete darkness.

After they had pulled her out of the cage, they stuffed her mouth with another ball gag, blindfolded her, and dragged her through a hall and down a flight of stairs. She was hoisted up with her arms stretched out over her head. The enema tube was a shock and it was incredibly agonizing.

We can't have you pissing or shitting during the show.

She replayed his ominous words over and over in her head. After the enema, they hosed her down with cold water. Nobody said a word to her, and she tried to fight but she was subdued by a solid punch to her gut. The blindfold never came off.

Now, she was restrained with metal cuffs on what felt like a wooden table. Her arms and legs were spread wide, stretched out and immobile. The table was tilted at an angle and she was facing forward. Her wrists throbbed with pain and they had covered her with what felt like a bed sheet. The last thing she'd heard was several sets of footsteps walking away, and then a heavy door being pulled shut and locked.

She was naked and in complete darkness and silence, alone with her thoughts. She was shivering with a level of fear that she never knew existed.

. . . during the show.

Whatever "the show" was, she knew that she was part of it. She had no idea when it was going to happen, or what they would do to her. She had spent her life in complete control of everything, but somehow it had all led to this point of complete helplessness. She couldn't stop quivering.

The situation overwhelmed her, and her tears turned to a high-pitched wail while in the midst of her pitch-black silence.

* * *

Everyone was in the living room making small talk and the room became quiet when Bruce and Marilyn stood up and asked for everyone's attention. Marilyn started:

"Thank you all so much for coming this morning. It's been so nice to get to know all of you and I'm sure we will continue that later, but we want to get started with the festivities. We really hope and think that you'll all get your money's worth as your darkest, deliciously sadistic fantasies are finally brought to reality at the expense of our two lovely guests of honor.

"We will begin with Sarah in the back yard. She's tied down over the barbecue pit and, I believe, Chris, that she's awake now?"

Chris nodded and Marilyn continued:

"Great. After Sarah, we'll all go straight to the basement from the back yard. Jennifer is down there right now, restrained and ready. She's also awake. When you enter the basement, you'll see a table with some masks on it. Just be aware that we'll be videotaping portions of Jennifer's torture so that we can sell it on the dark web and possibly recruit more clients if we decide to do this again. If you want to conceal your faces, feel free to put a mask on when it's your turn to go up and have your turn with Jennifer. You'll have free reign to go back and forth between the two girls and I am sure that Chris, our chef, would appreciate an extra set of hands every now and then."

Bruce continued:

"Now, very briefly before we go out, I'd like to acknowledge the men who really made today possible. These guys to my left, I can't even begin to describe the number of hours they spent watching the women, and ultimately putting their own lives on the line by kidnapping them for our enjoyment. Darryl, Hank, Tom, Willie, take a bow, my friends."

The guests clapped for Darryl and his crew.

"It was our pleasure and we all look forward to doing it again if we're asked to. We hope everyone enjoys the day," Darryl said.

"We sure will. Lastly, Chris is our chef for the day and he'll be handling Sarah," Bruce said.

Chris nodded as he received a round of applause.

"Without further ado, let's head out and get this party started!" Marilyn said.

She led the way with Bruce and as soon as the sliding door was opened, stifled screams could be heard in the predawn darkness. New York was in the middle of a heat wave, and it was hot and muggy even at the early hour. The group walked under the canopy and formed a circle around the barbecue pit where Sarah McConnell struggled, fought, and screamed for her life.

Chris stood next to a small table with two bowls and a basting brush on it. One of the bowls was filled with salt, the other, larger bowl was filled with his homemade sauce.

Marilyn said:

"As you all know, this is Sarah McConnell. Thirty years old, lived on Long Island. No children, and no family other than her mother and father. She graduated from Columbia University and Cornell, and then worked as a veterinarian. From everything that we could find on the Internet about her, she is, or should I say *was*, well-liked and very well-respected."

Marilyn continued as Sarah's screams and struggles escalated through her eulogy.

"She was watched for months and finally kidnapped late at night on her way home from work. Chris, do you want to tell us what is planned for her?"

"Sure. Obviously, she'll be cooked and served for dinner later. I anticipate that it'll take around twelve hours before she's ready to carve. Ideally you wouldn't cook a human being whole like this, but there is something aesthetically beautiful about it in conjunction with today's celebration, especially since she'll be kept alive as long as possible. None of that should affect the quality of the meat since the heat will be kept very, very low. She'll be dead for most of the cooking, unfortunately."

Sarah could hear everything, and she was already putting on a great show with a combination of screaming, crying, and struggling fiercely.

"There should be enough of her for everyone who wants to taste her. I'll also be serving sides of pasta salad, baked beans, and mac and cheese. I figure that this won't be for everyone, but I really suggest that you try it. The sauce is a rich honey barbecue sauce that I made from scratch, and we'll be applying it to her body throughout the cooking, so feel free to come out for fresh air later and help with that. You can also, if you like, take a few minutes turning her with the crank here. First, we need to rub salt on her. Does everyone want to help out with that?"

All six guests expressed interest.

"Very good. Her body is already very damp with sweat, so that'll make the salt stick. Front and back, hands down to her feet. Whose up first?"

"I guess we can do it according to auction bids. Howard, you're up first if you want to go," Marilyn said.

Howard gladly agreed. Chris handed him the bowl of salt, and he stepped into the pit and sprinkled some right onto Sarah's belly. Sarah was hyperventilating, no doubt realizing that she was being seasoned.

"Rub it in good! Get your hands dirty," Chris said.

Howard did as he was instructed, spreading it out evenly around her belly and vagina and massaging it in. Ruth was up next, and she rubbed some salt into Sarah's thighs. The rest of the guests, and then Bruce and Marilyn each got a chance to partake. Then Chris turned the crank so that Sarah was now looking straight down at the charcoal briquettes. They went in order again, and covered her entire backside.

"Alright, very good folks! Now a nice coating of the sauce and we'll be ready to get her cooking," Chris said as he turned the crank so that she faced up again.

Howard went first, picking up the large bowl and the basting brush and applying the sauce to her hands and her left arm. Ruth was next, and continuing what Howard started, covered the right arm with the sauce. The rest followed the same order and worked their way down her body until Marilyn, who went last, covered Sarah's feet. Once again, she was turned 180 degrees and her backside was thoroughly basted. Chris decided to leave her in that position so that she could see the moment the charcoal was lit.

With a charcoal rake, Chris repositioned the briquettes, spreading them out evenly underneath her. Everyone watched silently, completely caught up in the scene as Chris squirted lighter fluid into the pit and then picked up the long barbecue lighter. Sarah's eyes were wide open with fear, seemingly about to burst out of her head and her body wriggled furiously as she fought for her life. At this point she had to know it was a losing battle.

Chris lit the charcoal and the fire danced. He carefully monitored the flames, making sure they didn't rise too high. Sarah howled and screeched uncontrollably, instantly feeling the heat. Although it was kept low for cooking, it was still incredibly painful and already unbearable. When Chris was content with the fire, he took hold of the crank and slowly turned the helpless, squealing woman while everyone watched.

Wow.

Oh, my God.

God Almighty.

What a sight.

Good. Fuck this bitch.

I hope it doesn't take twelve hours.

"The crank will eventually get very hot, so we'll have some oven mitts ready if you folks want to come out and turn her," Chris said. "Low and slow is the name of the game."

Howard approached and asked for a couple of minutes at the crank. He savored the moment, turning Sarah as he ran his eyes over her body. Her fists were clenched, and the grimace of utter anguish on her face would be burned into his memory for the rest of his life.

The sight and sounds of an innocent, terrified woman being cooked alive was the most brutal thing any of them had ever experienced. None of them would have had it any other way. And with Jennifer awaiting their appetites for destruction as the finale, the very air itself seemed charged with orgasmic finality.

CHAPTER 29

THE SILENCE WAS FINALLY BROKEN when Jennifer heard another door burst open and several sets of footsteps entered the room. She couldn't tell how many.

She cried for someone to help her, but nobody said anything. She pleaded and begged, trembling uncontrollably. The footsteps stopped, and she heard a woman's muffled shrieking in the distance. Whatever they were doing to her, she was suffering brutally. Jennifer never knew that a human being could make such sounds--like a squealing hog being slaughtered.

Oh my God, Sarah.

Her respirations quickened when it dawned on her that whatever they were planning to do to her—the "show"—was happening right now. Her heart pounded in her ears and she began to hyperventilate.

They're going to kill me.

As she reached that realization, someone snatched the bed sheet off of her and she heard people clapping. She cried for help again, and then the blindfold was removed. Six people sat in chairs in front of her, and the four men who had repeatedly raped her were standing behind them. The couple that had given her water was standing to the left, next to a long table with a black sheet covering some assortment of objects. Straight ahead, between two of the chairs was a video camera on a tripod. The recording light was on.

Jennifer saw another woman and made eye contact with her, pleading with her for help. The woman smiled at her with cold casualness. Her eyes darted to each person, searching in vain for a friendly face, or at least a sympathetic one, but she saw only faces of heartless fiends. There was a mirror directly across from her on the wall and she could see herself naked, completely stretched out and restrained to the large table. She screamed through the gag for somebody to *fucking help her.* The woman standing to her left began to talk.

"The main event of the day, my friends. Jennifer Miller, Twenty-eight years old. As you can see, just a gorgeous, perfect body. Not married, no children, the only family was her mother and father. We found some info on her on the Internet as well. She was an athlete in college at the University of Connecticut. She was on the swim team and earned her degree in finance. She then worked as a financial planner for a prestigious Manhattan firm. She was successfully taken right out of her home in Queens. She appears pretty broken down now, but she was a bit of a fighter, quite feisty, really, and hopefully that side comes out again for your enjoyment.

"As we all agreed, our goal is to keep her alive for as long as possible. For the first two or three rounds let's stick to the non-lethal tools and then we can progress from there. The table can also be tilted to lay her flat on her back. Your choice, just let us know. Try to keep her from passing out, but if her body gives in to pain or shock, we have plenty of smelling salts to revive her. We have a hose to wash her off when she gets a little too bloody, so please leave her as clean as you can when your fifteen minutes are up."

Jennifer couldn't believe what she was hearing. She watched as the woman and the man ceremoniously removed the black cloth from the table. What she saw caused her to avert her eyes. The woman then held a camera in front of her face and flipped through photos of the missing 18-year-old girl, Jackie Nixon, taken in this same room. The last photo showed her slaughtered and butchered carcass hanging upside down.

Jennifer let out one more pathetic plea for help and then resorted to manic, delirious, uncontrollable sobbing. With tear-blurred eyes she looked back at the table. Along with the cattle prod there were several sharp metal instruments in what looked like a dissection kit; scissors, forceps, needles, and a scalpel. Next to the kit were sewing needles wrapped in a rubber band, pliers, hammers, nails, and nipple clamps. There was another open case containing an assortment of sharp knives and a bone saw.

Further down were what appeared to be some sort of electrical generator with alligator clamps connected to it, a micro blow torch, a nail gun, an electric stapler, a power drill, a large metal dental gag, packets of smelling salts, and a pile of small and regular sized towels.

These people weren't here to help her. Their faces were truly fiendish now, etched with pure, monstrous evil. Jennifer couldn't break free. Her body belonged to them now. She would be tortured and then murdered for their amusement. And there was no way out, no escape from that terrifying fate.

Sarah's distant shrieks seemed to be getting weaker but no less desperate. Jennifer closed her eyes. She tried to brace herself for what was coming and hoped that it wouldn't last long. She wasn't religious, but she closed her eyes and tried to pray. She didn't get much further than "*Please, God,*" before her attention was drawn back to the reality in front of her.

One of the men who was seated, the oldest one, got up and walked towards her. She was as helpless as an innocent fly caught in a spider's web. A very dark web. The man's eyes were as cold as a mid-Winter night, and they told a terrifying story.

I'm going to make you regret ever being born, those eyes said to her.

Please, God.

* * *

He saw Sean dozing off.

"Why don't you go home and try to rest a little. We'll keep you updated. The police are working on it. Let them do their jobs," Sarah's father said.

"I'm not going to work today."

"You should. Try to take your mind off everything."

"That's not possible. I want to wait until we get an update from the detective."

"Sean, that won't be for a few hours. The news outlets will start picking up on this soon and we're going to be hounded. You should go home, rest a bit and freshen up. We'll let you know if we hear anything."

Sean hugged Sarah's father and her distressed mother and got back in his car. Before he drove off, he picked up his cell phone.

"Hey, you've reached Sarah McConnell. I'm not available at the moment, but please leave a message and I'll call you back as soon as possible. Thanks!"

The cheerful sound of her voice made him tear up. He prayed that wherever she was she was okay, she was staying strong and fighting, and that she would be found.

* * *

Chris slowly turned Sarah McConnell over the open fire. It hadn't even been twenty minutes yet, but her skin was already turning slightly red. He was already sweating profusely from merely being near the heat. He couldn't imagine how much pain she was in.

"I think we'll get a couple of good hours out of you," he said to her.

Although she was gagged very well and her frantic blaring was incoherent, he knew what she was saying. She couldn't tolerate it any longer. She was asking him, begging him to kill her.

" *Prrrreee! Prrreee!*" she begged.

"Kuhh mme! Preee!"

"Please! Kill me please!" he laughed and mocked her.

"What would be the fun in that? These folks paid good money for you and Jennifer to put on a show. If it's any consolation, you'll be dead much sooner than she will. *Much* sooner."

He took the bowl with the barbecue sauce and applied a fresh coat, basting her breasts, belly and thighs. While he did that, he enjoyed the latest symphony of Sarah's muffled, but agonizing screams.

* * *

Howard was up first. He took one more sip of his wine, put a mask on and approached Jennifer. He had craved this moment for decades, and it was finally here. He looked right into her tear-filled, frightened eyes and gently rubbed her cheek with the back of his hand. He continued down to her chest and fondled her firm breasts. Her body was covered in sweat, and he felt her shaking and trembling. He moved his hand down between her thighs and gently rubbed the vulval lips, then pushed two fingers into her vagina. He loved the feel of the inside of this gorgeous twenty-eight-year-old woman, and the look on her face along with the sounds of her cries added to his delight.

"Non-lethal to start off with. Let's see," he said as he looked down on the table and mulled the choices.

He settled on the pliers. He traced her body with the jaws as she followed with her eyes. He zeroed in on a fleshy area just below her armpit, grabbed it with the pliers and slowly twisted. He focused on the pain displayed on her face as she wailed. He took his time and worked his way up her arm nice and slowly, grabbing any fleshy part and twisting. He was in no rush. He finished by twisting each of her breasts. He did the left first, then drew some blood from the right. He placed the pliers back on the table and wiped the small amount of blood off her nipple. Another dot of blood surfaced and he bent down to suck it off. Before he pulled his mouth away he clamped the nipple between his teeth and bit down hard, relishing the way it made her squeal and squirm.

He sat back down in his chair and watched as Ruth stood up to take her turn. She put her mask on and asked for the table to be reclined. Bruce honored her request, and the table was now lying horizontally, with Jennifer looking straight up at the ceiling.

"Would it be possible to have a bucket filled with water? And a cloth or a handkerchief?" she asked Bruce.

"Not a problem, just a second."

The lowest bidding guest left the basement to watch Sarah roast on the spit. Bruce took a bucket out of the closet, filled it up with water from the hose and placed it on the floor near Ruth. Marilyn returned from upstairs with a white cotton cloth and handed it to her. Ruth stretched it out and decided that it would do just fine.

She looked down at Jennifer and smiled. She went back to her seat, picked up her wine and downed it, then brought the empty glass back with her.

"Bruce, would you mind assisting me?" Ruth asked as she handed him the cloth.

"I'd love to," he answered.

"Good. I've read a lot about this technique since the war on terror started and I was always curious about it. All I need you to do is stretch that cloth out and hold it down nice and tight over her face."

Bruce followed her directions and Ruth filled the wine glass up with water. For the next fifteen minutes, they waterboarded Jennifer. After each pour, Bruce removed the cloth and watched as Jennifer gasped desperately for air. Following the second pour, the rest of the guests in the room walked up and surrounded the table to watch Jennifer struggling to endure the powerful drowning sensation. The metal cuffs loudly clanked against the table as she vehemently twitched and squirmed.

"That went by so fast. How unfortunate!" Ruth said when her fifteen minutes were up.

"You'll have quite a few more opportunities, I'm sure," Bruce said.

Bill, the professor from Penn State, now stood and approached the table.

"You can leave her flat like that. I've got something very special for her," he said excitedly.

The guest who had gone out to observe Sarah was now back as Bill was taking his turn. Bill picked up the bundle of sewing needles and removed the rubber band.

"Decisions, decisions," he said as he took one of the needles in his hand and held it in front of Jennifer's face. Her eyes, initially opened wide and drawn to the bundle, were now squeezed shut as she looked away.

"Fingers or toes?"

He walked around the table, staring down at her body, glancing at her hands and feet. He took one needle, made up his mind and took a firm hold of Jennifer's left foot. He guessed it was about a size seven, seven and a half. Working very carefully, he slowly inserted the tip of the needle up her big toe nail resulting in the loudest, ear-splitting shriek yet from Jennifer.

"Nineteen more to go, honey!"

One by one, he inserted the needle into each of her toenails on her left foot. She cried and howled as vociferously as her gag would allow, begged him to stop, but that only made him want to hurt her more. He'd had so many beautiful college students over the years, and had fantasized about having them at his mercy. Jennifer Miller, this New Yorker he'd never met, was his outlet. At this moment, he wondered if he was a monster whose heart was filled with evil. He did not feel an ounce of remorse as he tortured this innocent woman. If you were by nature a monster, how could it be evil? You were just the way God made you.

Yes, I was made this way. I'm not doing anything wrong. She *should have been more careful. It's* her *fault that she winded up here.*

He got to work on her left hand, pinning one finger at a time to the table and sliding the needle deep into each of her fingernails. He checked his watch, and knew that he had time to finish the last ten digits. He picked out a fresh needle to do her right hand and right foot.

Some of the guests couldn't help but wince through each of Jennifer's screams. She had no idea that she still had hours to go before she would be put out of her misery.

"Break time, people," Marilyn announced. "I think Chris could use a hand by the fire, and Sarah might not have much longer to live."

Bruce tilted the table forward to cause pain to Jennifer's wrists until the group returned. Marilyn blindfolded her again and left her to suffer alone as she led the guests outside to observe the live roasting of Sarah McConnell.

CHAPTER 30

EVERYONE TOOK TURNS BASTING SARAH. Some commented on the heat they felt on their arms while applying the sauce. The sun was up now, and Sarah had been over the fire for almost two hours. She was still very much alive, but her wild screaming had dwindled to an occasional whimper along with incessant sobbing. She had either accepted the circumstances or she was so exhausted and in so much pain that she simply couldn't fight anymore.

Chris was happy with the progress. Her skin was just a little darker shade of red now but not burning yet. The continuous basting kept the surface of her skin moist and relatively cool. There was still a long way to go, but she stayed alive longer than he thought possible. The guests took turns rotating her, and folding chairs had been set up so that they could comfortably watch Sarah's final moments while enjoying some refreshments; coffee, wine, beer, and a platter of cheese and crackers.

"She really is perfect for your first time trying human meat. Nice and healthy, not too thin but not out of shape. Really nice, thick thighs. Her legs are great. I'm very excited about how she'll turn out," Chris said.

"How long do you think, Chris? Do you still think about twelve hours?" Marilyn asked.

Sarah could hear the conversation.

"Yes, that's a ballpark figure. Once she's dead I'll raise the heat a little bit. But the body has to roast slowly so that it's done all the way through. I want her around one-seventy before she's taken down and carved up. Right now, she's probably at around one-ten or one-fifteen. The fire is very, very low but that's just to keep her alive. Once she's gone we'll really get the body cooking."

"Looks like she *might* be getting close," Bruce observed.

Sarah's eyes started to flutter and she appeared to drift in and out of consciousness. Chris continued to turn her, and the guests got up for a closer look. He reached in and lightly slapped her cheek to keep her awake. Her eyes slowly opened again and her mouth grew slack. Chris held the rotisserie in place with her face-up. Her body weakly twitched and jerked and her eyes flickered as the last bit of life began to fade away. Her eyes rolled up and she stopped moving.

"Is she gone?" Howard asked.

Chris reached down and pressed his thumb into her neck.

"She's barely alive. Very faint pulse," he said before licking a delicious combination of sauce and sweat from his thumb.

"I don't think she's coming out of this," Marilyn said.

"Probably not. I'd like to finish her off now," Chris said.

He walked to his minivan and came back with his butchering kit. He set it down on the table and opened it up. He turned Sarah face-down. Her body lightly twitched with what little ounce of life she still possessed. Chris took the very same knife that he'd used on his niece while his audience watched intently. He held it to Sarah's throat, and slowly cut across, making an incision deep enough to sever the jugular vein and the carotid artery. As she started to bleed out, her eyes opened wide and her body jerked. Her blood hissed and steamed on the hot coals. Her jerks slowed to spasms. Then finally she was still.

Her suffering was over. The cheery, vibrant, brilliant, and much-adored Sarah McConnell was dead. Much too soon, and with so much more to offer the world but for those assembled at this gathering, she served her purpose sensationally.

"Alright, I'm going to let the blood drain for a while and then I'll increase the heat. Not much left to do afterwards except turn and baste her. Any help with that would definitely be appreciated," Chris said.

* * *

Dr. Kevin Kramer arrived at work a little early on Monday morning. He had some paperwork to catch up on before the day started to get busy. He assigned one of the technicians to check on the animals that were lodged and while he was concentrating on getting everything up to date, the receptionist paged him on his office phone.

"Dr. Kramer?"

"Yes?"

"There are two detectives here and they want to talk to you. They said it's about Dr. McConnell."

"Okay, I'll be right out."

He felt uneasy as he went out to meet them. He wondered what was going on with Sarah and why detectives wanted to talk to him. He extended his hand and greeted the two men with handshakes.

"I'm Detective Roberts, Nassau County Police. This is Detective Williams."

"Kevin Kramer. What can I do for you guys?"

"Sarah McConnell works here, right?" Detective Roberts asked, holding up a photo of her.

"Yes, she's the night shift supervisor. Is everything okay?"

"She's been reported missing, sir. We want to confirm that she was here Friday and we'd like to talk to anyone who was with her."

"She's missing? Oh God, no. What happened to her?"

"We're not sure yet, but she hasn't been seen or heard from since Friday afternoon. Did she work her regular shift that day?"

"Yes. Yes, she came in Friday," Kevin said as he struggled to comprehend what was happening.

"Did you notice anything unusual? Did she get any odd phone calls or any visitors?"

"I left at four-thirty. Hold on one second, let me get one of her technicians on the phone."

Kevin retrieved his cell phone from his office and dialed Veronica's phone number.

"Veronica? It's Kevin Kramer."

He passed the phone to Detective Roberts who briefly questioned her about Sarah during her shift on Friday. Veronica confirmed that she was there for the entire shift, and that she didn't notice anything unusual with Sarah. She told the detective that she seemed like her usual happy self, and that she left work alone. Nobody came to pick her up.

"Thank you very much, sir. I'm sorry about the bad news," Detective Roberts said as he handed Kevin's phone back to him.

"Any way we can help, please let us know. Is there anything you can share with me? Do you think she's okay?"

"Honestly, we're not sure, but we believe it is suspicious. She doesn't seem like the kind of girl who would just skip town without telling anyone."

"Oh God. She's definitely not like that. She's a really, really good woman. She wouldn't hurt a fly. *Everyone* loves her," Kevin said somberly.

He shook the detectives' hands again as they thanked him for his help and left. He went back to his office and sat in complete disbelief. He got back on the phone with Veronica.

"Dr. Kramer, what's going on?"

"I have no idea. They said she's missing and they think it's suspicious.

God almighty, how could this happen to her of all people?"

Veronica started to cry and Kevin continued:

"I don't know what do to later, or for the rest of the week."

"I'll come in. I'll be all right," Veronica said.

"Just hold off on that, okay? I might close the place down for a couple of days. Let's see what else happens and what else we find out."

* * *

Jennifer's boss peeked into her empty office and checked the time. He walked down the hall to talk to Jessica.

"Hey, Jennifer hasn't come in this morning yet?" he asked.

"No, I haven't seen her."

"She didn't call or email or anything?"

"No, she was really out of it on Friday though. She looked like she was sick. Let me try to call her," Jessica said.

"Or maybe she started her fucking vacation early."

"Well, she's not picking up. Hey Jen, it's Jessica. Could you give me a call when you get this? Nick is wondering where you are. Thanks."

"Thanks, Jess."

"No problem, I'll let you know when I hear from her."

* * *

Howard patiently waited for his third turn with Jennifer. She was tilted forward again. The man who was up there now was nearly done stitching her cunt shut.

The whole morning continued to feel unreal and dreamlike. His fellow guests were all on the same page, torturing Jennifer very slowly while keeping her fully alert. The sounds of the screams coming from this woman were indescribable, but they provided quite a soundtrack.

"Hey, we're gonna get going," Howard heard Darryl whisper to Bruce.

"You sure, man?"

"Yeah, we've seen enough. It's a little much for us but everyone seems to be having a helluva time. We've already had our fun with her."

"Okay, sure."

"To each their own. No judgments here. We'll reconnect soon, yeah?" Darryl said.

"Definitely. Guys, thanks again."

Fucking wimps, Howard said to himself as he watched Bruce and Marilyn hug them goodbye.

As they left, the pussy stitcher was wiping a bit of spilled blood off Jennifer. Howard put his mask back on and approached her for his third round. He was going to make the most of this fifteen minutes.

"It's time to start getting serious," he whispered into Jennifer's ear.

She pleaded with him again. He loved the look in her eyes. He didn't know if she begged for release, or to stop, or to just put her out of her misery. Whatever it was, he didn't care. He had his fifteen minutes mapped out, and he got started.

Howard took one of the long nails and the hammer. He held the tip of the nail to the palm of her left hand, and drove it in with the hammer. She howled each time he hit the nail. Blood leaked from her hand, dripping down onto the floor. He took a moment to absorb her suffering, then drove another nail into her right hand.

She has to suffer. It's why our paths crossed.

He put the hammer down and picked up the nail gun. It was a good gun, a Dewalt Pneumatic capable of driving an eighteen-gauge two-inch nail at 200 pounds per square inch. He ignored her continued desperate cries and held it up against her left knee. He let his fingers linger on the trigger, feeling the power at his fingertips and enjoying his absolute authority over the woman. She made a screeching noise in the back of her throat that sounded like two cats fucking when he fired a nail into her kneecap with a loud thud. He savored the look on her face once again before he drove another nail into her right knee cap. He wiped some of the blood off her and then picked up the micro blowtorch, a Hot Devil. He pressed the igniter button and then adjusted the butane-fueled flame by turning the red knob on top. The torch flame sharpened into a fine point and he was ready to play with fire.

Howard made the most of his final minutes of this round, running the tip of the flame slowly around her body, circling her breasts then flaming her nipples before sweeping down her belly, pausing to blacken her navel and then heading between her thighs. She wriggled and thrashed in unspeakable pain. He held the flame to her freshly sewn labia. The stench of singed stubble and skin filled his nose. Jennifer bucked in full panic now but he kept the flame focused and saw the girl-meat sizzle and before he knew it, his fifteen minutes were up.

"I'm just getting fucking started with you," he said to her before he took his seat again.

Ruth put her mask on and approached Jennifer for her third turn. She sensed that Jennifer pleaded with her the most because she was a woman.

She must be thinking that whole "women are supposed to stick together" thing.

Ruth chuckled at that notion.

"Haven't you figured out that it's not going to work with me, darling?" Ruth said.

She was fascinated by the electrical generator and summoned Bruce. She asked him for help with it. He explained that it was a portable generator, and the alligator clips would emit a powerful electrical shock. He demonstrated by touching the tips of the two clips together, creating a horrifying display of fiery sparks.

"Oh my!" Ruth said excitedly as he handed them to her.

"They won't work individually. You have to touch them together if you're going to use them on her. You want to give it a try?"

"Oh, absolutely!"

"Good. Let me hose her down. It'll be more painful if she's soaked."

"Even better if you cover her with salt. It'll act as a conduit," Bill yelled from his seat.

"Then let's salt her up!" Ruth said.

While Ruth tested the clips, Bruce hosed Jennifer with water. Marilyn fetched the bowl of salt from the barbecue pit and poured it all over Jennifer's body, then they retreated to the back of the room and let Ruth have the stage for herself.

She touched the clips together again close to Jennifer's face. Jennifer winced and looked away when she saw the sparks.

"*Somebody fucking help me! Please!*" she yelled through the gag.

Ruth went in, touching the clips together and pressing them onto her chest, just above her right breast. Jennifer went silent as her body convulsed uncontrollably. Ruth pulled the clips away. A pungent curl of smoke drifted up from Jennifer's skin at the point of contact. She moaned, shuddered, and then Ruth hit her again in the belly, causing more violent spasms.

Ruth picked up the pace. She completely lost herself as she tortured the young woman, totally intent on administering one shock after another to various parts of the withering victim. She held the clips to the young woman's chest again, and pressed down hard as she felt the twitching body go still.

"Okay, Ruth!" Bruce yelled from the back.

Ruth removed the clips. Jennifer's head slumped down but her chest still slowly rose and fell. Marilyn picked up a pack of smelling salts from the table and held it under her nose.

"Welcome back, darlin'. You're not getting off *that* easy," she said when Jennifer snapped back into unwelcome consciousness.

"Okay, Bill. You're up."

CHAPTER 31

TARA NICHOLSON HATED MONDAYS. She was always sluggish in the morning and it took her awhile to settle in to the work week. Her busiest days as an accountant were payroll days and that wouldn't be until Thursday. She knew that if she got a leg up during down time and got ahead of things, it wouldn't be so bad.

Mondays are just the worst.

She walked across the office to file an invoice and then checked the time. It was just after eleven o'clock. Time for a cigarette break. She took the elevator down and walked outside to the corner where the smokers always gathered. She lit her cigarette, took her phone out and checked Twitter. She scrolled down her timeline and liked a few tweets. She scrolled further down, and her heart nearly stopped when she saw a retweet of an article from a Long Island news website, the accompanying photo catching her eye. She put out her cigarette and then clicked on the article.

SEARCH UNDERWAY FOR BELOVED VETERINARIAN, LONG ISLAND RESIDENT

Nassau County authorities are investigating the suspicious disappearance of a Mineola woman. Sarah McConnell, 30, was reported missing late Sunday evening after she had not been heard from since Friday.

McConnell, who is a chief veterinarian at an animal hospital in Manhattan, resided close to the home of a high school student who vanished in May. Jackie Nixon, 18, is believed to have been abducted and that investigation is still ongoing.

Although authorities have not officially linked the two disappearances, one law enforcement source, citing the proximately of the two women, stated that they are operating under the assumption that McConnell was also abducted, likely by the same person or persons responsible for the disappearance of Nixon.

No information on any suspects has been provided.

"We're in shock. She is the nicest, sweetest person you'd ever meet," a co-worker who wished to withhold her name said.

A press conference has been scheduled for 1 PM.

Tara looked at the picture of Dr. McConnell in the article. She was the one who had put her beloved kitty to sleep. Tara had felt compelled to write the Yelp review about her because she had been so graceful and compassionate. She sent the article's link to her husband, and he called her within two minutes.

"Oh my *God,*" she said.

"I know. I just read it. I can't believe it."

"Like, who would ever want to hurt that woman? So scary. We *knew* her!"

"I know. Hopefully they find her."

* * *

Lisa, the receptionist, answered the phone.

"Yes, hi. I'm looking for Jennifer Miller. Is she there? I've been trying her office phone but she doesn't answer."

"Um, no. Jennifer didn't come in today. Who's calling?"

"This is her mother. Did you say she didn't come in? Are you sure?"

"Yes, she's definitely not here. We were wondering where she was."

"Oh my God, we haven't heard from her. She texted me around four-thirty Saturday morning and said she was leaving town. She's not answering her cell phone either. She hasn't reached out to *anyone* there?"

"No, we thought it was really weird that she just didn't show up. Shit. Do you think she's okay?"

Jennifer's mother started to cry.

"I don't know. We just read a story about another missing woman. We've been trying Jennifer all morning. Oh *God!*"

"I just saw that too. You should contact the police right away. This doesn't feel right."

"Yes, we will right now. Can you take my phone number down and if you hear from her, *please* give me a call?"

* * *

Jennifer lost consciousness two more times and after they all had their fourth round with her, decided to let her get some stamina and life back before finishing her off. She was awake now but delirious and incoherent. Some of her bones were broken, and a few of her fingers and toes had been severed.

They retreated to the back yard and lounged in their chairs around the barbecue pit. The body of Sarah, now over three hours since her death, no longer resembled what once was a tall and striking Irish woman. The outer layer of her skin had caramelized to a rich deep brown and was very hot to the touch. Her gag had been replaced with a red apple and she now more closely resembled a whole hog roasting on a fire. There was small talk among the guests, ordinary folks talking about their normal lives outside of this gathering, but during periods of silence a faint sizzling sound could be heard coming from the roasting body.

"She might be done a little sooner than I thought. Can someone take over turning her while I get started on the side dishes?" Chris asked.

Bruce put the oven mitts on and took over at the crank. He looked down at the cooking body and remembered when she was first brought to the house. He remembered the thrill of stripping her naked, of her begging him and Marilyn not to hurt her. She didn't deserve any of it. She had lived a wholesome and virtuous life.

From all of that, to this.

Now, she was lifeless. The only sound coming from her was the sizzling and crackling of her smoldering flesh. Marilyn walked up to him with her phone and showed him the first article about her disappearance.

"She's already dead and they're just starting to look for her," Marilyn joked.

Bruce laughed and looked at the picture of her. She was smiling and holding a cat in the photo. Now here she was: dead after a brutal ordeal, an apple stuffed in her mouth.

* * *

Jennifer slowly began regaining her bearings. Her whole body throbbed and pulsated with different levels of excruciating pain. It had been a long time since she'd heard those horrible sounds coming from Sarah. She figured that she was dead, and she prayed that her turn would come soon. She couldn't believe that she'd let herself be kidnapped and that now all hope was gone. No one was coming to save her. She was going to die, and she couldn't take the suffering anymore.

She thought about her parents and wondered if they knew that she was missing yet. She thought it might be better if they never found her body, so that her poor mother wouldn't have to think about what she had endured and how much she suffered. She closed her eyes and cried while thinking about her parents and her life as a whole. How short it had been and how fast it had gone.

Terror and dread rushed through her when she saw the group return to the basement. She knew now that the man's name was Bruce, and he approached her.

"Your friend out there is barbecuing up *beautifully.* If by some miracle you're still alive, I'll let you eat a piece of her," he said.

Fucking choke on her.

The group took their seats, and Jennifer took several deep breaths. She tried to summon the strength to endure the final moments of her life.

They'll be caught. They won't get away with it. Please don't let them.

* * *

Howard approached Jennifer again. She appeared to have regained some of her spunk. That pleased him since torturing a semi-conscious woman would be rather pointless. He reached into the dissection kit and took the scalpel. He had a feeling that this would be his last shot, so he wanted to make it most memorable.

He sliced away the thread that had sewn her vagina shut. He pulled the needle out of her skin and tossed it onto the floor. He put on a pair of latex gloves and got started on what he envisioned would be his grand finale. He stuck the blade of the scalpel into her vagina and twisted it.

Oh yes, she's back.

Jennifer's hysterical shrieking pierced the air and blood poured out as he slowly cut away inside, performing an impromptu genital mutilation.

"Scream for me, bitch!"

The blood flowed out onto his gloved hands and onto the floor during a melody of frenzied screams. Howard stopped because he didn't want to kill her and ruin it for everyone. He tossed the blood-soaked scalpel onto the table and let the gloves drop to the floor. He took the hose and sprayed her pubic area, then wiped it down. The bleeding wasn't going to stop, so he stuffed her vagina with a hand towel. As his finale, he used the electric stapler to hold the rag in place against her skin.

It was now Ruth's final moment and she intended to pay homage to her recently departed husband. She asked for the dental gag to be inserted into Jennifer's mouth.

"Just kill me please! I can't take anymore! *Please!*" she hollered to Ruth when the ball gag was removed.

Bruce and Marilyn quickly inserted the dental gag, which forced

Jennifer's mouth wide open. Ruth picked up the pliers from the table. The guests leaned forward in their chairs, knowing what was coming. For fifteen minutes, Ruth slowly pulled out as many of Jennifer's teeth as possible. She put one of the teeth into her pocket and let the rest fall to the floor. Blood from Jennifer's mouth trickled down her body.

When Ruth was done, Jennifer had only a handful of teeth left. Bruce and Marilyn removed the dental gag and wrapped a roll of duct tape around the back of her head and mouth several times, gagging her and forcing her to drink her own blood.

Bill was next. He picked up the power drill.

"It has been an absolute pleasure, Jennifer," he said before he started what he imagined to be his final turn.

He drilled into each of her kneecaps and elbows, causing her to lose consciousness again. Once again, she was immediately revived. When she was brought back to life, Bill drilled into each of her shinbones.

Without any doubt, they were all getting their money's worth.

* * *

"C'mon you two, finish her off!" Bill yelled.

The guests agreed and applauded the idea that Bruce and Marilyn, the architects of this unforgettable day, should have their moment with what was left of Jennifer Miller. They should be the ones to send her to the afterlife.

Amazingly, they ended up getting a sixth round and that's when they began removing pieces of her body. The bone saw severed her legs below her knees. She lost consciousness again, but they kept working the body, subtracting piece by bloody piece. Her breasts came off smoothly, slid off her torso and hit the floor with wet splats. The rest of her fingers were chopped off. When her eyes flickered open again, they were gouged out with a knife.

Now, Bruce and Marilyn would end what little was left of her life. She had passed out but still had a pulse. Bruce took one of the knives. He and Marilyn held it together as they plunged it into Jennifer's stomach. Together, they cut downward just as they had done with the wedding cake on the day of their marriage. Bruce took over and gutted her while she still had life left. Jennifer Miller took her last breath, and her head slumped over as her intestines slowly poured out onto the floor.

A rousing round of applause filled the room. This collection of people, previously strangers, celebrated the successful torture and murder of Jennifer Miller. It was an event that would keep them connected for the rest of their lives.

And now it was time to enjoy the cooked flesh of Sarah McConnell. Outside at the barbecue pit they refreshed themselves with beer and wine while they waited.

Chris predicted another thirty minutes. He had been checking the temperature of the meat frequently and decided to increase the heat. Over the fire, what was once a human female was now largely unrecognizable. The skin on the body was beautifully crisping and crackling and the mouthwatering, sweet and savory aroma of barbequed flesh wafted through the air.

The mood among the guests was exuberant. They chatted excitedly and helped set the table with plates, utensils, and the side dishes.

Bill, the college professor, tapped his bottle of beer with a fork and said:

"Before we eat, I just wanted to thank Bruce and Marilyn one more time. For them to come up with this brilliant idea and make it a reality, and to share it with us in their home, really amazing stuff, you two. And to the rest of you who made it, this couldn't happen without you. We all realized the risk involved, but we all took that leap of faith and I think I can speak for all of us when I say this was better than I ever could have imagined. Guys, you *have* to do this again!"

Bruce and Marilyn smiled through another burst of applause and thanked everyone.

"We will most definitely consider another event. But we haven't gotten away scot-free just yet. The police are going to be looking *hard* and we don't *think* they'll trace anything back to any of us, but you never know," Bruce said.

Marilyn added, "Yes, we'll want to wait awhile. We want to edit the video of Jennifer and sell it, and see what kind of response we get from that. We'd love to do this as often as possible but Bruce is right, we need to be careful and prudent. There will be a lot of coverage about the girls in the coming weeks, so stay aware and if anyone gets questioned, let us know right away."

Chris extinguished the fire and announced, "Time to eat, folks. Bruce, could you help me carry her over?"

The two men donned oven mitts and on the count of three, they each lifted one end of the rotisserie and carried Sarah's sizzling body to the table, laying it out on the cutting board. They cut the twine that bound her wrists, elbows, waist, knees, and ankles and slid the rotisserie out from under her.

The guests, in order starting with Howard, lined up while Chris carved the choicest cuts of the body and placed it on their plates. As they feasted on her flesh, everyone agreed that Sarah tasted as good as she had once looked.

EPILOGUE

TUESDAY AUGUST 1, 2017

Roger Farrell was a sanitation worker in Dallas, Texas. He was twenty-four years old and just starting out with his first steady full time job. His parents had talked him into working for the city because of the benefits. They found him his own apartment and paid his rent for the first six months until he was able to take care of it himself.

The job didn't pay well, but it paid enough. He walked into his apartment after an overnight shift. Normally, after such a shift, he'd take a shower and go right to sleep. But not today. Today, he went right to the computer because he had done everything that was required of him and his payment had gone through. The link was finally there.

He turned the computer on, took his boots and pants off and grabbed a bottle of lotion, setting it down on his computer desk next to the keyboard. He logged in to his desktop, opened up Google and typed in "Jennifer Miller New York". The results were a host of articles about her disappearance, as well as the other two New York women. He clicked on the article that had his favorite picture of her. It looked like a regular Facebook profile photo. She was in a bar, smiling and holding a cocktail. Her hair was straight. She looked gorgeous.

He minimized the window and adjusted the page so that the only thing showing was the photo. He zoomed in, then slid the window to the left of his computer screen. Her beautiful eyes, full of life, were looking right at him. Her smile shined through the screen. Next, using the special software, he logged in to that message board on the dark web. In his inbox was what he had paid $1,000 for. It was a video clip with the file name "jennifermillertortured". He'd saved up for it and he wouldn't be able to pay his rent next month, but this was going to be worth it. He clicked on the message from "SadisticMistress34":

Roger;

We received your payment. Thank you very much. The link to the Jennifer video is below. It's 30 minutes long. Please make sure no one is around when you click it, and I'd suggest wearing headphones too so that there is no chance any neighbors can hear it. The screaming in this is VERY loud, hopefully to your enjoyment.

Other than that, all is well here. We're laying low for now but we will keep everyone informed about any future events.

Thanks again, and enjoy the video!

Roger clicked on the link which allowed him to download the video. He held his cock as he looked at the smiling photo of Jennifer and watched the download progress bar. Ten more seconds. He resized the window to fit perfectly into the empty space at the right of his screen, right next to the photo.

He put his headphones on, and clicked "play." He lathered his member with lotion and got started, nice and slowly. He wanted to make it through the entire video. The video began with a masked man pulling a bed sheet off a table that had been tilted horizontally. There she was.

Holy fuck . . .

It was definitely her. He compared the photo on the left to the face of the terrified screaming woman on the right. No doubt, Jennifer Miller, that missing New Yorker all over the news, was the woman on that table. A minute later, another masked figure was hammering nails into her hands. Roger winced with each strike of the hammer. When he felt that he was getting closing to finishing, he slowed the pace down.

The video then cut to another masked figure. This one was smaller, but every bit as vicious. This person was torturing Jennifer with alligator clips, her body convulsing as each shock was delivered. He glanced again quickly at the photo on the left, listening to the incredibly loud screaming as he looked at her smiling.

He checked the timer on the video. It showed 8:10. There was no way he would ever be able to afford a live show (should they do another one in the future), but this was more than sufficient for him. He didn't think he could physically do this to a woman, but he sure as hell enjoyed watching others do it.

He had 22 minutes to go and it was already so, so good.

* * *

SATURDAY AUGUST 12, 2017

The guests spent the night at the Hudson Valley house and helped with the massive cleanup the day after the gathering. The kind gesture was unnecessary but greatly appreciated by Bruce and Marilyn. Ruth was wearing a necklace she had fashioned from Jennifer's tooth. It was only for the day and she knew it would need to be discarded, but she enjoyed it immensely.

Two burn barrels had been needed. The skeletal remains of Sarah McConnell along with her organs, her clothes and personal belongings were thrown in one of them. Jennifer Miller's remains and her clothes were placed in the other. While the two fires burned side-by-side, the guests helped to clean up the basement.

The chore took nearly twenty-four hours of constant hard work, but they got the job done. All evidence was completely erased and the basement was cleaner than it had ever been. The ashes from the barrels were dumped in a wooded area twenty miles away. The women, while alive, were caged next to each other. Now their ashes were disposed of together.

News reports were closely monitored for the next several weeks. Federal authorities got involved once Jennifer Miller was confirmed missing. Friends and families of the women appeared frequently on television, pleading for their safe returns.

So far, no one connected with the kidnapping and murder of the girls had been questioned. The police had nothing. During a joint press conference with the various law enforcement agencies involved in the case, women were warned to be vigilant and completely aware of their surroundings at all times.

"We suggest that you don't use earphones. Put the phone away until you safely arrive at your destination. Walk in groups whenever possible. Just be aware, and be smart, and you'll be fine," a law enforcement authority said during one of the press conferences.

Bruce and Marilyn printed their favorite article. It had photos of all three of the women smiling. They framed it and hung it up in the basement.

* * *

drake1100: Hello?

SadisticMistress34: Hi, how are you?

drake1100: Very good. Your information was passed along by a mutual friend who was at your event. I'm definitely interested in buying the Jennifer video. I've heard that it is really making the rounds and it's amazing.

SadisticMistress34: Oh? Thank you! Yes it was. I only wish the day could have lasted longer.

drake1100: Been following it all in the news. They have nothing.

SadisticMistress34: I know. We've been keeping current on the news as well. It's looking good.

drake1100: Yes it is. I know that you are probably going to lay low for a while, but if you are ready for more, I might have a business opportunity for you.

SadisticMistress34: I'm listening . . .

drake1100: I have many contacts overseas. Russia, the Middle East, quite a few countries. There are slave operations that would pay top dollar for American women. Very serious, and a lot of money.

SadisticMistress34: Really . . .

drake1100: Yes. Everyone is tired of filthy prostitutes. They would pay a lot more money for something new. An American girl would yield a fortune if one of the oil tycoons in the Middle East wanted to buy her. You can imagine why. You appear to have the means to kidnap them, and I have the means to ship them overseas. We will split everything 50/50. Think about it, and get back to me when you are ready.

SadisticMistress34: We certainly will, my friend. I think we can do business.

ALSO BY GIL VALLE

GIL VALLE
WITH BRIAN WHITNEY

RAW DEAL

THE UNTOLD STORY OF NYPD'S "CANNIBAL COP"

A MEMOIR

"One of the most twisted tales you will ever read."
—Patrick Quinlan, Los Angeles Times bestselling author of **SMOKED**

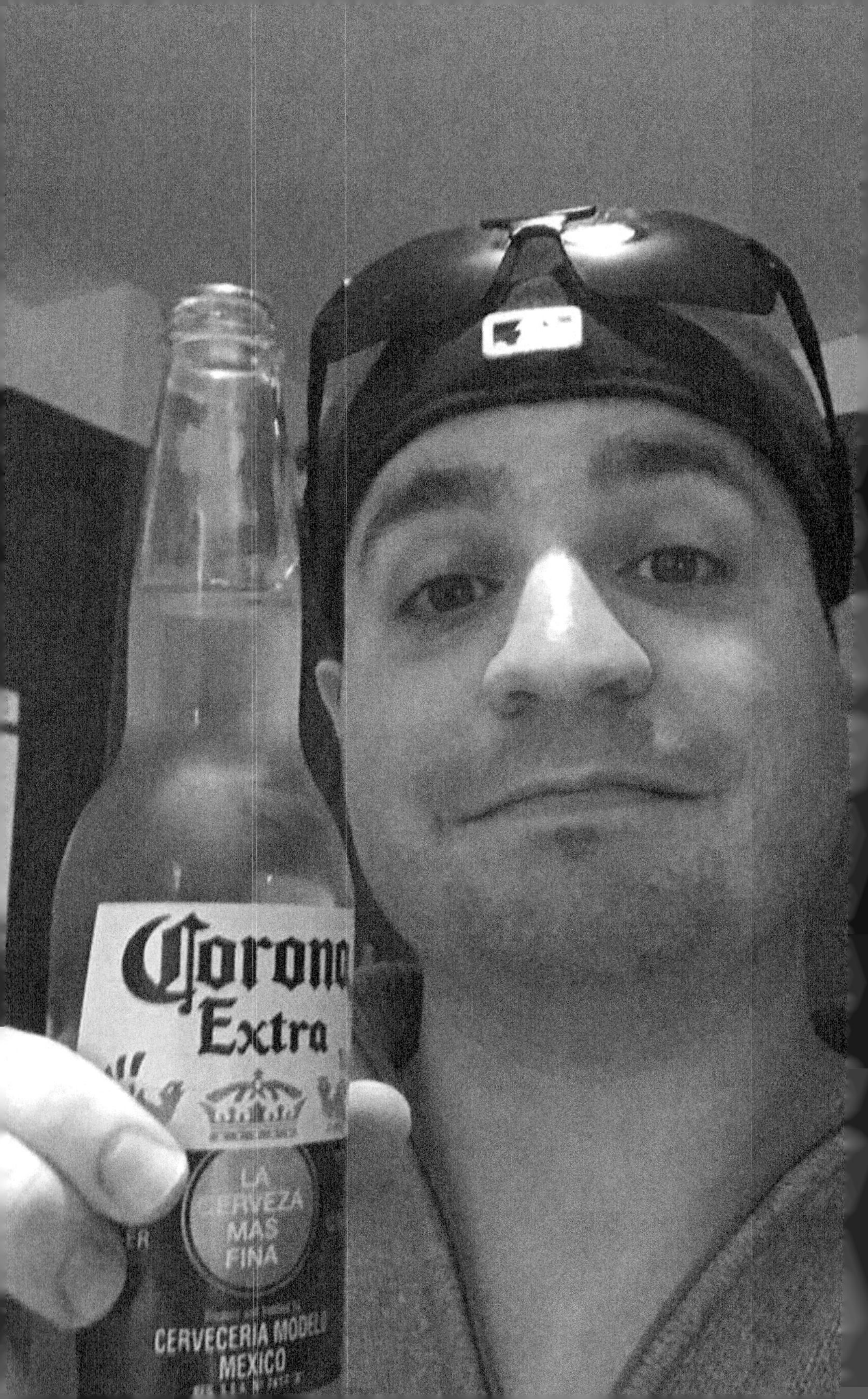

Extra
LA
MAS
FINA
CERVECERIA
MEXICO

Gil Valle is a former NYPD patrol cop who rose to infamy in 2012 after he was wrongfully arrested by the feds for allegedly plotting to kidnap, cook, and eat women. He became known to the world as the "Cannibal Cop" and faced life in prison. Valle has since been completely exonerated of all wrongdoing and he released *Raw Deal*—a memoir about his ordeal and the criminal case—in February, 2017.

After *Raw Deal*, Gil realized that he enjoyed the process of writing a book. Since he got simpleminded FBI agents to believe that his fictional stories on the Internet were actually the workings of a massive cannibal conspiracy that spanned three continents, he felt that it made sense to try to make fictional writing into a new career. Gil sent his first extreme horror manuscript to Red Room Press (Comet Press) and was excited to receive an offer within a week. He plans to continue writing.

Gil Valle resides in Queens, NY with his two dogs Dudley and Tyson. He considers himself a good cook and actually does consume food. He has appeared on Inside Edition, Crime Watch Daily with Chris Hansen, People Magazine, Cracked.com, Slate, The New York Post, The New York Daily News, The New York City Crime Report, True Murder with Dan Zupansky, and many other places.

Twitter - @gilvalle3
Instagram - @gilvalle14
Facebook - https://www.facebook.com/gil.valle.7

RED ROOM
EXTREME HORROR MAGAZINE
OCTOBER 2017

ISSUE 1 FEATURES

FICTION BY

JACK KETCHUM
MEG ELISON
TIM WAGGONER

INTERVIEWS

MEG ELISON
AUTHOR OF THE BESTSELLER
THE BOOK OF THE UNNAMED MIDWIFE

GIL VALLE

Printed in Great Britain
by Amazon